GHOST HUNTING

GHOST HUNTING

True Stories of Unexplained Phenomena
from The Atlantic Paranormal Society

JASON HAWES & GRANT WILSON
WITH MICHAEL JAN FRIEDMAN

POCKET BOOKS
New York London Toronto Sydney

Pocket Books
A Division of Simon & Schuster, Inc.
1230 Avenue of the Americas
New York, NY 10020

First Pocket Books trade paperback edition October 2007

POCKET and colophon are registered trademarks of Simon & Schuster, Inc.

For information about special discounts for bulk purchases,
please contact Simon & Schuster Special Sales at
1-800-456-6798 or business@simonandschuster.com

Designed by Carla Jayne Little

Manufactured in the United States of America

10   9   8   7   6   5   4   3

Library of Congress Cataloging-in-Publication Data
Hawes, Jason.
Ghost hunting : true stories of unexplained phenomena from The Atlantic Para-
normal Society / by Jason Hawes and Grant Wilson with Michael Jan Friedman.
        p.   cm.
ISBN-13: 978-1-4165-4113-4
ISBN-10:   1-4165-4113-6
1. Ghosts. 2. Parapsychology. I. Wilson, Grant. II. Friedman, Michael
Jan. III. Atlantic Paranormal Society. IV. Title.
BF1461.H377 2007
133.1—dc22   2007016062

To Kristen Hawes, my wife, for helping me make T.A.P.S., which was a dream of mine, a reality. And to Samantha, Haily, Satori, Austin, and Logan, my children, for showing me how enjoyable life's little moments can truly be.

—Jason Hawes

To my amazing wife Reanna Wilson, for her eternal love and support, and to Connor, Noah, and Jonah, my boys, for giving every action I take purpose.

—Grant Wilson

Authors' Note

Because paranormal activity is not supported by conventional scientists or by specialized equipment manufacturers, it cannot be re-created in a controlled setting. Therefore the field of paranormal investigation is populated by theory, speculation, and opinion. Due to these limitations, what is shared within these pages is what T.A.P.S. as an organization feels is closest to the truth. T.A.P.S. is not claiming these beliefs to be fact; rather, they are presented as educated theories and observations based on years of experience and research.

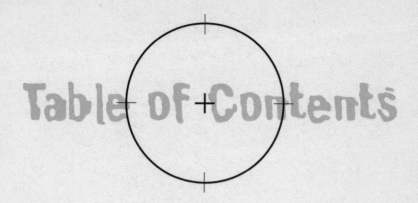

Table of Contents

GHOST HUNTING

BY JASON HAWES

At The Atlantic Paranormal Society (T.A.P.S. for short), we typically start our investigations with a question: Does this case merit our attention? The answer is usually dependent on a second question: Does the person who believes he or she has paranormal activity truly need our help? That's our primary goal—to help.

If people think they've seen a ghost, heard an unexplained noise, or found things moved out of place and they're concerned about it, we'll pack up our vehicles, bring in our equipment to document the activity, and, if necessary, even bless the place. We do believe there are supernatural entities, both benign and destructive, but before we accept that a house or building is haunted we check out every possible angle.

I'm inclined to be especially sensitive to those clients

1

who see paranormal phenomena and believe they're losing their minds, as I'll explain in a moment. But the decision to go on a job is not mine alone. It involves my partner, Grant Wilson, as well. Grant and I developed T.A.P.S. together, so we rely on each other's perspectives. He's like a brother to me and has been almost from the day we met.

At the time, I was twenty-two, a couple of years removed from my first paranormal experience. At the age of twenty, I had gotten involved with a lady who practiced Reiki, a Japanese technique for stress reduction, relaxation, and healing that depends on the manipulation of a person's life-force energy.

At first, I was skeptical about the idea of life-force energy. Then, after six months or so of exposure to the technique, I started seeing things. Usually it started with a mist, out of which emanated a dim light, and then out of the light came other things—including see-through animals and full-body human apparitions.

I would point them out to whoever was with me, but no one else seemed to see them. They looked at me like I was crazy, and frankly, that was how I looked at myself. I felt like I was honestly and truly losing my mind.

It was scary as all get-out. I didn't know where to turn. Then a friend introduced me to a guy named John Zaffis, who was known as a paranormal researcher in Connecticut. Zaffis ran some tests and determined that I was becoming sensitive to paranormal phenomena.

That was a whole lot better than going crazy, but it was far from comforting. I was still seeing things I didn't want to see. And Zaffis, who lived three hours away, couldn't work with me as often as I would have liked. At his suggestion, I started the Rhode Island Paranormal Society, which came to be known as RIPS.

It wasn't a ghost-hunting organization like T.A.P.S., at least not at first. It was more of a support group. I was trying to connect with people who had gone through experiences similar to mine, hoping they could help me deal with my sensitivity and shut it off. I ended up meeting people all right, many more than I would have imagined.

But none of them knew how to help me.

Then, one day in the aquarium at Mystic, Connecticut, a woman in her fifties came up to me out of nowhere and asked in a tender, almost intimate way, "How are you doing?"

It was a strange question to ask someone she had never met. Before I could answer her, she continued. "Hon," she said, "you're seeing things, I know. But you can make it stop. Try green olives. I'll see you again soon." Then she walked away. I was too dumbfounded to stop her and ask her how she knew about my problem.

Stranger still, the green olive approach worked. I ate those suckers all day long, a bottle a day, and the visions I'd been having went away. I wasn't cured for life, because whenever I stopped eating olives the visions came back. But at least I had found a way to alleviate the symptoms.

In the meantime, my RIPS group had taken on a life of its own, blustering its way into graveyards and abandoned buildings with a couple of cameras, a tape recorder, and a whole lot of optimism. We caught a few EVPs now and then, but I can't say they were anything of merit.

EVPs, by the way, are electronic voice phenomena. When a ghost hunter enters a room, he always asks any paranormal entity for a sign of its presence. Even if an entity is there, listening, and inclined to answer, its response isn't always audible to the human ear. Sometimes it can only be picked up on a sound recording device and discovered later on, when you're going over your tapes or digital impressions.

EVPs have been part of the paranormal investigator's repertoire since their inadvertent discovery in the 1950s by a man recording birdsongs. To his surprise, he got human voices instead.

The other thing RIPS seemed to capture a lot was orb activity. An orb is a round, translucent, mobile packet of energy thought to signal supernatural activity in some way. However, people often mistake naturally occurring phenomena like dust, bugs, light reflections, and condensation for orbs. It wasn't at all uncommon for someone in RIPS to "prove" a haunting because he had caught some "orbs" with his camera, when in fact they'd been floating particles of dust and there hadn't been a ghost within fifty miles of the place.

RIPS also visited some homes, responding to residents who wanted to know if they were living with supernatural entities. I remember one Connecticut case in particular—not because of any significant paranormal activity but because while I was there I ran into the woman I had met in the Mystic aquarium. Like us, she was checking out the house for signs of haunting.

It was a strange moment. But then, she had said we would meet again. I made sure to thank her for the olive idea.

About that same time, I got a call from a guy who had seen our rinky-dink RIPS website and said he could improve on it, make it nicer-looking and more functional. In fact, he was willing to redesign it for free. He just wanted to add it to his portfolio so he could get other work in the future.

It was a hard deal to beat. I met with him at a local place called Bess Eaton Doughnuts. I remember him bringing his good friend Chris. I also remember wondering if it was really the website he wanted to talk about, because the conversation kept drifting off in the direction of personal experiences with the paranormal.

It was outside the doughnut place, as we were talking alongside my Subaru, that the guy finally came clean. He had had an experience of his own—a recurring one, from the time he was fifteen until he turned seventeen and went to college. An intense experience in the heavily wooded part of Rhode Island where he had been raised. And every once in a while, the experience still popped up.

The guy was Grant Wilson.

His friend Chris verified everything he said, mentioning tests he and Grant's other friends had put him through to determine if his experience had been real. I'd be more specific, but Grant doesn't like to say much about what happened. It's kind of a touchy subject with him.

Anyway, our conversation left the parking lot and continued in my living room. We sat there for hours discussing our philosophies about the paranormal, and we found a lot of common ground. This went on for days, then weeks. Finally I said, "Screw the rest of what's out there," referring to other ghost hunters and their methods. "Let's do it our way."

You see, most groups then—like now—were running around saying everything is haunted. They didn't worry about collecting evidence. They just walked into people's houses, got in touch with their feelings, and decided there were ghostly presences afoot. In fact, they never found a place that *wasn't* haunted.

Grant and I insisted on a more rational approach. Before we would ever say a place was home to a supernatural entity, we needed to have proof. It was a significant departure. And it was on that basis that we founded T.A.P.S.—both of us, because the idea was as much Grant's as mine.

Grant said it best: "If you set out to prove a haunting, anything will seem like evidence. If you set out to disprove it, you'll end up with only those things you can't explain away."

Right from the beginning, we found people with similar philosophies. Our T.A.P.S. website (designed by Grant, of course) got two hundred hits a day, at a time when that was a pretty impressive number. And the total kept climbing. Two years later, we were up to two *thousand* hits a day.

Other groups looked for publicity, seeking out the media on Halloween and so on. We never did that. But we still wound up building a substantial network of like-minded ghost hunters, people who were inclined to approach the supernatural with a certain amount of discrimination.

And soon we weren't just getting calls from people in the New England area. People were reaching out to us from California and Michigan and Louisiana. Unfortunately, we didn't have the money to travel out there and help them, and we also didn't have reliable contacts in other parts of the country to whom we could refer them..

Grant and I decided that in order to extend our contact network, we first had to separate the people who saw things our way from those who didn't, and the best way to do that was by being controversial. So we put up an article on our website that essentially said orbs were trash.

Now, orbs were really popular in those days. Hearing they were insignificant was, for some people, a slap in the face. They railed back at us, telling us we were crazy, and the battle was on. The paranormal field was polarized almost overnight.

But we found the people we were looking for.

The first one was Al Tyas at D.C. Metro Area Ghost Watchers (affectionately known as D.C. MAG). Al saw things the way we did and became a big part of the T.A.P.S. extended family. We got support from other places as well, across the country and even overseas. People from Europe, Asia, and Australia were contacting us to thank us for taking a stand.

As our network continued to expand and our organization grew, Grant and I cut a deal. He would take care of the creative and technical facets of our organization, areas where he's the undisputed king. I would handle the management and business aspects. Among my responsibilities was making sure we brought the right people into our group on Rhode Island.

One was Brian Harnois. When he first showed up, he was like a big kid, full of that gee-whiz kind of passion, and he had already formed his own ghost-hunting group of three to four people. He believed in orbs, vampires, you name it, but he was also a clean-living guy who didn't mind rolling up his sleeves and doing the dirty work.

The more he got to know T.A.P.S., the more he liked what we were doing. Before long, he convinced his group to join us. As it turned out, Brian was the only one of them who ended up sticking with us.

Anyone who has seen *Ghost Hunters* is familiar with Brian's shortcomings. For one thing, he likes to spin yarns (also known as lies), and it drives us crazy. All he really wants to do is make people like him, but it backfires.

He used to be our case manager, a job we gave him because of his enthusiasm. As such, he was the one who fielded calls from people in distress. He brought to each case the organization you'd expect from a former member of the military police, but he also got on our nerves—mine in particular.

Brian is easily excitable, thinks everyone needs immediate help, and never considers the distance we're going to have to travel before he commits us to an investigation. Also, he's perpetually wide-eyed about ghosts. Just the sight of what looks like an orb on a videotape can make him declare a place is haunted.

On the other hand, Brian's enthusiasm has a plus side: it drives his work ethic, and I can count on him to see to the equipment. Well . . . usually. There was the time he forgot the chairs for an all-nighter at a lighthouse, and at another site he somehow lost an expensive piece of technology.

But at heart, he's okay. I know he's dedicated to our mission. And we're a family, so we forgive each other's mistakes. Sometimes it's my job to remind everyone of that.

Carl Johnson joined T.A.P.S. around the same time as Brian. Carl is a suave, well-mannered, articulate retail salesman who also happens to be a demonologist. By the time he came to us, he had already racked up years of experience investigating the paranormal. He had a habit of bringing a briefcase with him everywhere he went, which wouldn't have been so weird if it hadn't been empty half the time.

We were pleased to have Carl on hand, and even more pleased when his twin brother, Keith, came aboard. Keith is a born-again Christian and much more religious than his brother. He's also a walking encyclopedia. We'll be driving to an investigation with him and pass a college campus, and suddenly he'll sing me the school song, or relate some obscure fact about the second cousin of the school's founder.

"How did you know that?" I'll ask. And he'll tell me it was a *Jeopardy!* question back in March of 1983. On the other hand, he's also prone to giving long explanations of things when short ones will do, and his voice is so soothing it can put you to sleep.

Then there's Steve Gonsalves, a police officer from western Massachusetts. The first time we spoke to him on the phone, he asked to join T.A.P.S. We liked what he had to say and how he said it. The problem was he lived two hours away. We advised him to start his own group instead.

For a while, we lost track of the guy. Then we heard about this New England paranormal group that was doing great work in Springfield, Massachusetts—maybe even better work than we were. When we contacted them, thinking we could learn from each other, we found out their leader was Steve Gonsalves!

He's since become a part of our primary investigative team, but he still runs New England Paranormal as a member of the T.A.P.S. extended family. Steve's a real down-to-earth, dependable guy. As you'll see, we trust him one hundred percent—even if he does have a few inconvenient phobias. Fortunately, one thing he's not afraid of is ghosts.

Donna LaCroix, another mainstay of our organization, came to us about four years ago. An environmental engineer, she had gone to high school with Grant and was looking for help with some paranormal experiences she'd had growing up. Grant talked her through her issues on the phone. Before he was done, she was asking to join the group.

It was a good thing. Donna turned out to be a whiz at case management. She came in and reorganized the whole process. She's also accompanied us on quite a few cases. She doesn't like to hold equipment, and it's a constant struggle to move her into the realm of the scientific, but she looks after us when we're on the road, making sure we eat right and that we go to bed when we should.

Donna has shown a clear sensitivity to the supernatural, so she gives us another perspective in an investigation. She's also a terrific interviewer, not only in terms of her ability to sympathize with the victim but also because she can smell a fabrication a mile away—and we've run into our share of fabrications.

Of course, there's more to T.A.P.S. than the team I lead with my buddy Grant. We have another fifteen members in Rhode Island and probably the same amount conducting investigations for Steve Gonsalves in Massachusetts. They're the ones who work behind the scenes, taking care of the confidential cases we would never show on television.

The arrangement works for them because their jobs prohibit them from being publicly associated with a paranormal group. These people work for NASA, the CIA, and the FBI. They include a forensic scientist, a nuclear physicist, and even a Secret Service agent, but they're so dedicated to ghost hunting they don't mind doing it anonymously.

So T.A.P.S. has plenty of talent we can bring to bear, and

plenty of experience. But the heart of the organization is still my partner Grant, whom I affectionately call G.W. He's the one who designed our investigative protocol. He's also the one who gets the lay of the land in each case, making sure before we set anything up that we know where cold drafts may enter, where noises may originate, and what obstacles may exist. After all, we have to operate in the dark, and expectation and excitement can make people careless.

Grant's always questioning what people think they see or hear. One thing he notices in the correspondence we get is how often people claim they've captured the faces of demons in their photos. This is often the result of "matrixing," or the tendency of the human brain to see familiar features in complex shapes or colors. (That also goes for hearing voices in ordinary sounds.)

Pictures that contain complex shapes and variations are the most likely candidates for the overactive imagination, Grant's discovered, as are "features" that look like those of cartoon characters. He has art training, so he can tell right away if something has the right proportions to be a face. He advises others to keep this in mind when trying to decide if a mysterious image in a photo is a human expression.

And of course, there's always the possibility that a photo has been faked. Digital photography has made deception easier and more prevalent, so we're extra careful about reportedly demonic or apparitional photographs.

Grant's driving passion is to make paranormal investigations more scientifically acceptable. Me? Even with the evidence in front of me, I'm pretty skeptical. So we balance each other out.

"What makes us click," Grant once observed of our partnership, "is that we're total opposites." He sees me as the doer—the brawn of the team—and the stick to his carrot. We're at different ends of the interpersonal relations spectrum. When I'm annoyed with someone, he can show up and mix in some understanding. And when he's soft with people, I don't hesitate to say so.

Grant and I are also partners in a different way. We work together as plumbers for Roto-Rooter, the largest provider of plumbing and drain cleaning services in North America. If you own a home, there's a good chance you've used Roto-Rooter at some time in your life.

I got into the business first, then brought Grant in as well. At first he was reluctant because he was trying to build a career for himself in computers. Now he's grateful that I got him into the right kind of hardware—the kind that involves a wrench and a long copper pipe.

Come to think of it, that's *two* good turns he owes me for.

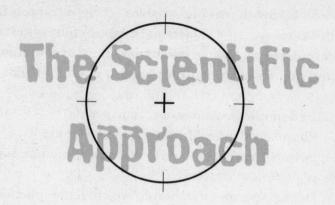

The Scientific Approach

BY JASON HAWES

Throughout this book you'll hear us talk about the scientific approach to ghost hunting, so let me explain what that means. Scientific knowledge comes from systematic and objective observations, which help us make deductions we can trust. It also means we have to test those deductions through controlled experiments that can be repeated by others under the same conditions. After subjecting phenomena to recording, measurement, and experimentation, we may realize that our initial observations were in error, or we may see more evidence to support our hypothesis. But the point is to try to debunk it first.

Once we have some patterns that support our hypothesis and lack patterns that would contradict it, we can proceed with our next step. If an experiment can't be brought into a lab to control for all possible variables (obviously, ghosts fall into this category), the subject must be carefully observed in different types of settings and under different conditions. In doing this, we're trying to accomplish several things:

- Determine the causes of certain events
- Eliminate all possible natural explanations
- Define a core essence for the phenomenon from regularities
- Define specific situations involving the phenomenon
- Learn what the phenomenon does under other conditions, such as after prayer or when it is clearly addressed with questions
- Predict what the phenomenon might do if it were moved away from the venue in question

In every investigation, we collect a wealth of data through different types of cameras, meters, and voice recorders, and from observations and reports of strange experiences. We sift through all of this as objectively as possible before we begin to draw conclusions.

We understand that ghost hunting isn't an exact science. We have to accept the fact that we're working in a real-world setting. However, we're determined to come as close to scientific accuracy as we possibly can. That's the only way we're going to produce reliable evidence and advance the study of the paranormal.

The Cases

BY JASON HAWES WITH GRANT WILSON

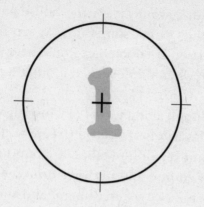

POWERFUL FEELINGS
JANUARY 1996

Sometimes it's not just a supernatural visitor that's plaguing a residence. In at least one case we came across, the problem was also someone else.

Mary and David Green, who owned a house in western Massachusetts, asked T.A.P.S. to help them with a spirit that kept moving objects in their home, creating unwanted light shows, and making pennies appear on the floor of their younger son's room.

The couple also told us that they were hearing noises, as if people were going up and down their stairs. They would find themselves sitting upright in their beds in the middle of the night, having been awoken by wild laughter or the sound of a toy piano being played in their attic—even though they didn't own a toy piano. On occasion, they saw a shadowy figure standing at the foot of their sons' beds.

Sometimes they would leave the house and have to go back because they forgot something. When they returned through their basement door, they would hear what sounded like a party. But when they checked it out, there was no one around.

Grant and I took along two of our investigators, Andrew and Rich, to Massachusetts. David Green, we found, was an imposing six–and-a-half-foot-tall, 300 pound rock crusher. As we interviewed him and his wife—who seemed to snipe at each other a lot—we set up cameras and audio recording equipment in all the house's reported hot spots.

Our first inkling that there was genuine activity in the house was when Grant and I saw the figure of a man walk by an interior doorway that led to the kitchen. When we got up to see who it was, we couldn't find anyone there.

It wasn't long before the pennies materialized in the younger boy's room. Six of them, scattered on the floor, just as Mary had described. Try as we might, we couldn't figure out how they had gotten there.

Later, at around 3:30, Grant and I were sitting in the living room with Mary when several faint blue lights from about three feet to six feet in height began to whip around the room. We watched them, spellbound, until they faded away.

Before we could discuss what we had seen, we heard a clunk and saw a good-sized rock come bounding down the stairs into the living room. It kept rolling until it was right in front of us, then stopped like a trained cocker spaniel. Mary had witnessed the light phenomenon before, but not anything involving a rock.

Deciding that this would be a two-night investigation,

we packed up our stuff and said that we would return the following evening. When we came back, we brought along Jodi Picoult, a writer friend of ours, to see if she would experience what we had experienced.

Once again, six pennies appeared on the floor of the boy's bedroom. Then, while walking up the stairs, Andrew felt something move by him. The temperature in that spot dropped ten degrees. Later, Grant heard footsteps following him.

By four in the morning, we had accumulated dozens of hours of video and audio footage and were almost ready to leave. We were assuring Mary that we would call her as soon as possible with our findings when Andrew's flashlight, which had gone missing, rolled into the room—and turned itself off. As we tried to understand what we had seen, the batteries for the flashlight rolled in after it.

Clearly, there was something going on. We were eager to get back to Rhode Island, go over our recordings, and see what we may have picked up. As it turned out, it was quite a bit.

First of all, there were EVPs that coincided with each appearance of the six pennies. One of them sounded like a voice saying, "Fine, take it."

But the most interesting evidence we found was in one of our infrared cameras, with which we had recorded a conversation with Mary in her attic. She'd been talking about her husband, and it had been clear that she wasn't happy with him. As she spoke on the video, bright lights began to swarm around her, multiplying until we could barely see her face.

Then the subject turned to her kids and she seemed to

relax. At the same time, the lights faded away. But when she spoke of her husband again, they returned—with a vengeance.

We went back over our notes and reached an interesting conclusion, which we presented to Mary and David when we returned to their house. As far as we could tell, all the activity in the house was revolving around Mary. David had even mentioned he never experienced problems when she wasn't around.

Grant and I said there was no way to know exactly what role Mary and her frustrations were playing in the house's array of paranormal activity, but it was possible that she was acting as a beacon, attracting spirits to her home. It was also possible that she was somehow causing objects to move subconsciously, a phenomenon we had heard of but never encountered ourselves.

Having spent two nights in Mary and David's house, it was obvious to us that their marriage was in jeopardy and the animosity in the home was adding fuel to the supernatural fire. Later, we got in touch with Mary in an effort to help her control her ability.

Soon afterward, Mary and David obtained a legal separation from each other. At that point, the paranormal activity in the house abated.

GRANT'S TAKE

What really bothered us about this case was that a child was involved. Jason and I both had soft spots in that regard because he had a couple of kids already and I was starting a family of my own. Our wives didn't like the idea of being without us at night, especially when we had to travel to another state, but they understood in this instance.

THE WOMAN IN THE CLOSET
FEBRUARY 1997

Sarah and Donald Wrenn lived in a big, four-bedroom house so that their kids could have lots of room to be kids. But something was plaguing the Wrenn children night after night. The couple called in T.A.P.S. to find the source of the problem and see what could be done about it.

Grant and I made the trip to southern New Hampshire to help the Wrenns, along with a couple of T.A.P.S.' earliest members, Paula Silva and Andrew Graham. Andrew, who had helped with the Green investigation, was a kid from New Hampshire who was going to school in Rhode Island. He had a big heart and would do anything to help. One time he got a huge splinter in his hand during an investigation and managed to finish the case anyway.

While Andrew and I set up the equipment and walked

through the house, Grant and Paula interviewed Sarah and Donald. Their children were asleep, but they were able to describe the kids' experiences.

Karen, Jesse, Adam, and Ellen, who were ten, eight, seven, and five years old respectively, were having nightmares pretty much every night. The three older kids had told their mother they'd seen black shadows in their rooms. Ellen, the youngest, claimed to have spoken with someone named "Irma," who lived in Ellen's bedroom closet.

Sarah and Donald were worried. They wanted to know who Irma was and why Ellen had adopted her as a friend. They wanted to know why their kids were seeing shadows in their rooms. Put simply, they wanted to know what the hell was going on.

Sometimes you can wait all night to find evidence to support a homeowner's claims. Sometimes the evidence eludes you altogether. That night at the Wrenns' house, Andrew and I ran into something even before we finished setting up.

We were in the hallway positioning a video camera when we found ourselves confronted by a dark mass. I tried to get it on camera, but the battery was dead—even though it had been charged a few minutes earlier. Spirits need energy to manifest themselves and they'll take it from anywhere they can find it. In this case, it seemed to come from our camera battery.

Sometime later, as we were exploring the house in teams, the motion detectors in the kitchen went off. A moment after that, the one in the hallway near the bedrooms went off as well. Then we heard a loud bang.

When we investigated, we saw both girls hiding under their covers. Karen told us that she had been roused from sleep by a huge bang on her bedroom door. We noticed that the girls' closet was open even though it had been closed when they'd gone to sleep.

In order to calm the girls down, Sarah told them the bang had been one of our cameras hitting the floor. Karen and Ellen seemed to accept that and went back to sleep. But an hour later, Karen ran out of her room babbling about her closet.

Grant and I went to investigate. We saw that Ellen was still fast asleep, but in the recesses of the closet, a dark shape that looked like a woman was sitting on some cardboard boxes. The air in the room was oppressive—warm and thick, like the hottest summer days.

We moved closer to the entity, confronting it. The shape seemed to tilt its head as if to get a better look at us. Then it vanished—but not before we got a sense of its all-too-human features.

We described what we had seen to Sarah, who went pale and suggested that the entity might be her great-aunt, who had passed away months earlier. In fact, now that she thought about it, the activity in the house had started at about the same time that they'd acquired her great-aunt's belongings.

"Where are they?" I asked her.

"In the basement," she told us.

We went downstairs to see what might have been included in the deceased woman's belongings. As we descended, we heard what sounded like footsteps following us down the stairs. And as we approached the pile of stuff Sarah had described, Grant and I felt ourselves being pushed from behind, which was jarring to say the least.

As it turned out, the woman's belongings were nothing out of the ordinary—mostly clothes. However, they were important enough to Sarah's great-aunt to keep her tied to this world and the Wrenns' house. We suggested to the family that they get rid of the dead woman's stuff and have their home blessed.

They did as we suggested, placing their great-aunt's belongings in storage and asking a priest to bless their house. Immediately after that, all activity in the house ceased.

GRANT'S TAKE

What was odd was how the two boys in the house, Jesse and Adam, slept through everything that happened that night. Motion detectors went off and we heard that loud bang, and the girls woke up—but not the boys. I can only speculate that the dead woman had more of an affinity with Sarah's daughters than with Sarah's sons.

STAND BY ME
FEBRUARY 1997

Most of the ghosts we encounter in books and movies are ghosts of people who lived—and died—a long time ago. They were alive during colonial times, or during the Civil War, or in the Victorian era. That's what we as a culture have been conditioned to expect from ghostly visitors.

Indeed, many of the supernatural entities Grant and I have encountered have their roots in those bygone times. But not all of them. Some of them are of a much more recent vintage.

When Casey and Dan Kelly agreed to house-sit for their friends in a two-level house in northern Rhode Island, they had no idea what they were getting into. It started when Casey heard what sounded like a male voice in the room where her four-month-old son, Liam, was sleeping. Concerned, she got up and went to check on the child, but there was no one else in the room.

The scenario repeated itself the next night, and the night after that. At the same time, Casey began to feel a presence in the house, as if there were someone lurking just out of sight, watching her. Finally, she caught what she believed was a glimpse of the intruder out of the corner of her eye.

He was a young man with dark hair, dressed in a blue T-shirt, jeans, and white Converse sneakers. Though Casey wasn't old enough to remember the fifties, it was a look she associated with that era. Over the next few days, she saw the figure again and again, always with her peripheral vision.

Finally, the Kellys called T.A.P.S. Grant and I went out on our own and spoke with the couple. We discovered that Dan hadn't seen or heard anything out of the ordinary. The experiences were strictly his wife's. Casey didn't seem especially frightened by the phenomena, but she was concerned about the safety of their child.

Because they were only house-sitting, Dan felt it wasn't their place to remove the entity, if it came down to that. On the other hand, they were supposed to remain in the house another three weeks, and he felt that his family life was being disrupted. Young Liam had gotten very attached to his mother in the preceding few days, and he cried uncontrollably whenever Casey left his side.

Grant and I set up a camera in the living room facing the hallway where Casey said she had seen the entity. Then we walked through the house, instruments in hand, alert for voices or other signs of a haunting. Unfortunately, we came up empty.

Finally, around two in the morning, Casey cried out. When Grant and I responded, she said that she had seen the entity again, out of the corner of her eye as usual. He was standing in the hallway, dressed the same as always.

We reviewed the videotape in the camera and didn't see any sign of a human figure. However, we did see a flash of light and a collection of floating globules. Obviously, something had happened at that moment.

The rest of the night was uneventful. It seemed to us, based on everything we had heard, that if there was a spirit in the house it was a harmless one. After all, it hadn't done anything threatening. It just seemed to be curious about the baby and the new people in the house.

When we followed up a few days later, we learned that Casey had been in contact with the homeowners and had told them what transpired. They were a little shaken by the information. Apparently, one of them had had a brother who had died in his early twenties during the 1950s. Eventually, they showed Casey a picture of the young man. He was exactly as she had described him.

Grant and I encouraged Casey to reason with the spirit by explaining her family's situation out loud and asking it politely to remain hidden until after the Kellys left. Casey did and the incidents stopped—until the day she and her family left the house. Then she saw the entity one last time, as if it were saying good-bye.

GRANT'S TAKE

People often look at us strangely when we tell them to communicate with the spirits haunting their homes. But sometimes it's the only way to make a house livable again. If you had a neighbor who was doing something bothersome, you would talk to him, wouldn't you? It's the same with a ghost.

THE GHOST IN THE WALL
MARCH 1997

A s Grant likes to point out, if a phenomenon occurs in only one spot, it's most likely not of supernatural origin. The supernatural just isn't that meticulous.

That's the first thing that occurred to us when Eric Small and his girlfriend, Tara Quinn, pointed out the lone wall from which they had heard voices and banging sounds every night. The couple also said they had been pushed into this wall against their will by an unseen force. However, they hadn't seen, heard, or felt anything anywhere else in the house.

Had we known in advance how localized the occurrences had been, we might have thought twice about making the four-hour trip to Hackensack, New Jersey, where Small and Quinn lived in a 1950s-era, cottage-style, two-bedroom home.

But hey, we were there already. It would have been silly not to go ahead with the investigation.

Besides, these people were obviously distraught over what was happening. We don't like to abandon anyone in need of help.

There were four of us representing T.A.P.S. at the house—Grant, me, an investigator named Brian Drevens, and Bethany Aculade, our group's clairvoyant at the time. While Brian and I interviewed the couple, Grant and Bethany checked out the place and set up our equipment—which wasn't difficult, given the concentrated location of all the occurrences.

I couldn't help noticing how the couple's story seemed to change during the interview. At first, I thought they were simply confused. Then, when we were talking to them individually, we got conflicting accounts. Something fishy was going on.

Meanwhile, Grant and Bethany found a number of books on the subject of hauntings under the bed in the master bedroom. This struck them as strange—not just that the couple was reading such books but that they had hidden them from view.

A little while later, Brian went into the basement to look around and saw what appeared to be gray speaker wires going up into a wooden joist. The other end of the wires went into a back room that had a padlock on the door.

We decided to keep all this to ourselves for the time being and see what the night had to offer. Right about the time Small mentioned, the noises began—and as he had claimed, they were all in the vicinity of the wall. Ghostly voices. Banging sounds. But they were flat somehow, missing the accompanying vibrations.

That was when we asked the couple about the speaker wires in the basement. Small and Quinn seemed to become defensive at that point and refused to let us into the back room. The tension mounted as we insisted.

Finally, they opened the door for us. The room contained a tape recorder, which was feeding banging noises and ghostly voices into a speaker embedded in the wall. You can imagine how ticked off we were.

Small said he had tried to fool us in order to get his house on *Sightings,* a popular TV show in the 1990s that investigated the paranormal. He pointed out that George Lutz, the owner of the "Amityville Horror house," had made millions off his experience once it was chronicled in a book and then a movie. Small wanted to ride the same gravy train—at our expense.

GRANT'S TAKE

Unfortunately, the Small situation isn't unique. We have found there are lots of people out there seeking to scam us in order to cash in one way or the other. Our best safeguard is the T.A.P.S. philosophy we established on Day One: Make sure you rule out the normal before you concede the possibility of the paranormal.

HIGH-RISE HAUNTING
NOVEMBER 1997

Dealing with the occult can be a nasty business. The key is to remember that malevolent spirits don't just show up in a house—they're invited by something one of the residents did. Usually, it's an innocent act, a case of someone dabbling in things he doesn't understand. But sometimes we have to wonder if the invitation might not have been a conscious one.

By the time we got a call from the owner of a Toronto apartment building, he was frantic—so much so that we could barely make out what he was saying over the phone. All we could hear was "golf balls."

After we calmed him down a little, he started to make more sense. Apparently, he and his tenants were being tormented by a storm of paranormal activity. Doors were opening and closing on their own. Furniture was moving, keeping people from getting into their apartments. People kept hearing growls and other noises at all hours. And in one apartment, a box of golf balls insisted on emptying itself, the balls rolling into the form of an arrow.

"What should I do?" the owner pleaded.

"Don't follow that arrow," I said, as we started pulling things together for a trip up north. Obviously, this was a situation that had to be addressed immediately. "We'll be there tomorrow."

It took us a few hours to gather a team of five, which included Keith Johnson, Andrew Graham, and Bethany Aculade, as well as the necessary equipment. By driving all night, we were able to arrive in Toronto the following morning. As we pulled up in front of the building, which was a high-rise, we were glad we had allotted ourselves three days to cover the place. Even then, we might be pressed for time.

It turned out that the disturbances had mostly taken place on the tenth floor, and the owner already had an idea of where the problem had originated. He showed Grant and me into apartment 10C, from which a tenant had been evicted for failure to pay his rent. The place was full of occult symbols. Some of them were carved into the wooden furniture. Others were painted on the bedroom walls in fluorescent colors, visible only when we flipped the switch and activated a black-light bulb.

Every room had different-colored bulbs. In the dining room and kitchen they were red, giving those rooms a really morbid atmosphere. There were also occult books and magazines all over the place, including some that contained the writings of Aleister Crowley—an occultist in the first half of the twentieth century who had been called "The Wickedest Man in the World."

In talking to the other tenants on the tenth floor, we learned more about the apartment of the evicted man. The lady across the hall, who owned a Chihuahua, told us that her dog had started barking uncontrollably at the door to 10C one day. As she went to pick him up, she saw the door open—on darkness, since there was no one there. Then, without warning, it slammed shut, prompting her to wet her pants in fright.

Five people said they had seen a six-foot couch stand on its end, manipulated by unseen forces. They had also witnessed the golf ball phenomenon in 10C, with the balls forming an arrow that pointed into the tenant's bedroom. A maintenance man had seen the refrigerator in the apartment slide out of its place and throw its doors open. People who had entered the apartment of the evicted man out of curiosity had smelled bad odors from time to time and discovered scratches on their bodies where there hadn't been any before.

The other tenants were spooked, to say the least. They were moving out of the building in droves. In an attempt to keep them, the owner had had a Catholic priest bless the place, but the exorcism hadn't obtained the desired effect. Keith Johnson, who is a priest himself, explained that if an exorcism isn't conducted in a strategic manner, the entity in question can still find a way to hang on.

Over the course of three nights, we went over 10C, its neighboring apartments, and the common areas of the building with every device at our disposal, and we experienced much of what the residents had experienced. Lights went on and off. Doors opened and closed. Furniture moved by itself. Members of our T.A.P.S. team caught electronic voice phenomena that appeared to be words spoken in Latin.

At one point, Grant and I were exploring 10C when we heard the sound of hammering, which seemed to be coming from the bedroom. But when we opened the door and followed it in, we heard it coming from elsewhere in the apartment.

What might have been the most shocking demonstration of the paranormal was the golf ball formation. Right before our eyes, the box opened and the golf balls came rolling out over the kitchen floor. Before they were done, they had formed a perfect arrow pointing to the bedroom. There was no slope in the room, so that couldn't have been the explanation for it. Those balls just rolled on their own, as if they knew what they were doing.

Personally, I hate it when objects move on their own. It gives me the creeps like nothing else can.

One conclusion seemed indisputable: there was an inhuman entity infesting apartment 10C. The evicted man had opened some sort of doorway, allowing a malevolent spirit to enter his domicile and take charge of it. If we could evict it, the building would probably return to normal.

But as we had pointed out to the owner, an exorcism had to be carried out in a certain way if it was to do any good. With the owner's approval, Keith blessed the place with holy water, starting with the four corners of the building in order to keep the malevolent spirit from escaping the premises. Then he blessed the rest of the high-rise, one apartment at a time.

In the process, members of our team reported feeling scratched, slapped, and pushed. And paranormal activity wasn't abating in 10C. But Keith pressed on. Finally, he got to the source of the trouble. As he blessed 10C itself, dishes and glasses started falling from the cabinets in the kitchen and shattering on the floor. Then, all of a sudden, the activity stopped.

It was quiet in the apartment. As far as we could tell, the entity was gone.

We had one regret as we left Toronto: though we had caught some of the paranormal activity with our cameras, we had to turn the tapes over to the owner of the apartment house in accordance with his request. What's more, we understood. If the results of our investigation had ever gotten out, he wouldn't have been able to rent an apartment in that building ever again.

GRANT'S TAKE

I'll never forget that nice old lady with the Chihuahua. She was genuinely scared, and with good reason. No one was happier than she was when the activity ceased and the building got back to normal.

UNHOLY SPIRITS
FEBRUARY 1998

We look to our houses of worship for shelter in spiritual matters. But what happens when a house of worship is itself haunted?

That was the question in front of us when a pastor in eastern Connecticut called T.A.P.S. to investigate his old Baptist church, which was rife with seemingly paranormal activity. He first got an inkling that something was amiss when he heard laughter from the mezzanine during one of his sermons. Although the church was full at the time, he was the only one who heard the strange laughing sound. It chilled him, but he convinced himself that he had misheard. Then it happened again, and it continued to happen.

When he was busy in his office, he would hear the sounds of a crowd in the chapel. But when he went to check out the noise, he saw no one. Lights turned on late at night, seemingly of their own volition. One time when the pastor arrived at the church early, he found most of the free-standing pews stacked in front of the main chapel doors.

From the vantage point of a playground across the street from the church, parents pushing their kids on swings would see a winged creature standing next to the church entrance—and it didn't look like an angel. Its wings were sloped downward, like a demon's.

Clearly the pastor had a problem, one he couldn't dismiss. The final straw was when he was standing in the chapel and saw some man-shaped shadows approach him, then fade away. It made him wonder if there was something evil in his church, something that needed to be addressed—and soon.

When our team arrived, we found the pastor to be a kindly, soft-spoken gentleman. He and his maintenance man gave us a tour of the church property, which included a walk through an old Christian graveyard. We would have to investigate that as well if we were going to do a thorough job.

As we returned to the church, the pastor mentioned that the building was old, but he didn't know exactly how old. In fact, he didn't know very much of its history. We made it our business to do some research in that regard.

As two of our people continued to interview the pastor, Grant, Keith Johnson, and I set up our equipment in the chapel and the mezzanine above it. We didn't have to wait long before we started seeing the types of activity the pastor had seen.

At about 12:45 a.m., the motion detectors we had left in the mezzanine sounded an alarm just as the temperature in the chapel plummeted some twelve degrees. A knocking sound traveled rapidly around the perimeter of the chapel from one end to the other. And soon after, Keith recorded an EVP from the mezzanine that sounded like people marching.

At around 2:00 a.m., we were all in the church's rec room. One of our members went into the chapel to retrieve her EMF detector (a piece of equipment that measures variances in the electromagnetic field), which she had left there, and she witnessed three apparitions dressed in outdated clothing—all of them male. We rushed out into the chapel to join her, too late to see the apparitions. But we could hear faint sounds of many people moving about.

At the same time, one of our members who was checking out the graveyard caught sight of an entity walking through it. It looked to him like a soldier. When he approached it, the entity appeared to dissipate.

The evidence was mounting that we weren't dealing with one supernatural entity but many. The question was *why*. What had happened in that place to tie so many spirits to it? Why were they still there?

The next day, we began our research—and found some answers. It turned out that the church wasn't the first one to stand on that property. Another church had preceded it— one that was had been used as a refuge for soldiers returning from the Civil War. Unfortunately, that earlier church had caught fire one night, and many of those sleeping inside it had perished in the blaze.

Sometime later, the current church was erected, built on the original foundation. That was why we had heard the sound of marching. We were dealing with the spirits of Civil

War soldiers. At the pastor's request, Keith blessed the place and set the spirits free. The activity ceased immediately.

GRANT'S TAKE

We maintain a relationship with the Catholic Church, which has priests dedicated to addressing supernatural activity. Usually, we're calling on the church for help. This time, it was the other way around.

POSSESSED
MAY 1998

When Nora and Timothy Sawyer called T.A.P.S. in a panic because their daughter Emily was cursing a blue streak and throwing heavy furniture around the room, one word kept coming up over and over again: Possession.

Everyone who has seen the movie *The Exorcist* knows about possession. An individual is taken over by a demonic entity, often through no fault of her own. The victim may babble, fall prey to seizures, display marked changes in personality, or demonstrate superhuman strength.

Emily Sawyer was doing all of the above.

When our T.A.P.S. team arrived at the Sawyer house in Falmouth, Massachusetts, nine-year-old Emily was dragging furniture around her bedroom and swearing like a sailor. It took all four of us—Grant, me, Andrew Graham, and a

Catholic priest—to restrain her. It wasn't easy, either. We didn't want to hurt her. We just wanted to evict the demon inside her.

As the priest began the rite of exorcism, Emily was still twitching and spasming, her pupils dilated, her hands curled into claws. Her face was a battleground, reflecting the forces writhing inside her. As fathers, it tore us up to see a child in such torment. Finally, the rite was completed and she went limp.

By then, we were pretty limp too, our clothes damp with sweat. But our job wasn't done. It's not enough to chase the demonic spirit from its host. You have to cleanse the whole house.

As the priest and Andrew opened doors and blessed all the other rooms in the house, Grant and I sat down with the family, which included another daughter—a sixteen-year-old named Annie. They told us they had been experiencing other phenomena besides Emily's bizarre rampages.

There were drastic temperature changes in the house, usually from cold to hot. Growls could be heard in the hallways and in the basement. From time to time, they smelled dirty diapers in the girls' bedrooms.

The adults said they had seen objects moving on their own—candles sliding, chairs falling over, and the chandelier spinning in the kitchen. Annie, on the other hand, seemed reluctant to talk about the moving objects. Grant and I got the impression that she was holding something back.

When we pressed her, she admitted that she and her friends had begun using a Ouija board and dabbling in black magic. However, she said, she hadn't gotten her sister involved in any way. Her parents went nuts, demanding to know the extent of what she had done and why she hadn't told them about it.

As they argued, Grant and I saw dark masses appear and slink around the hallway and the bottom of the stairway. The temperature in the room was rising noticeably—nearly fifteen degrees, according to our instruments. Up in her bedroom, Emily began to foam at the mouth.

Calming everyone down, Grant and I explained to Annie what she had brought into the house. When it comes to the occult, the younger members of a household "belong" to the older members and can be placed at risk by the older members' actions. So when Annie had taken part in black magic, she'd dragged her sister in with her, and it was Emily who was paying the price.

It was critical that Annie stayed away from the occult from that point on, or her sister would be placed in jeopardy again, exorcism or no exorcism. Responding to what was essentially a wake-up call, Annie agreed to steer clear of black magic. She just hadn't realized the demonic trouble she'd been inviting.

Unfortunately, the trouble wasn't gone yet. It continued to rage as our friend the priest blessed one part of the house after another. The chandelier in the kitchen spun around, all the doors in the hallway swung open and closed, and two more black masses appeared in the corners of rooms.

Finally, the priest had blessed every area in the house except the girls' bedrooms. As he got to work there we experienced heightened activity, including crazy temperature swings and difficulty breathing. At one point, I was slapped in the shoulder by something I couldn't see. Grant was grabbed around the middle.

The priest was feeling the entity's resistance as well. However, he hung in there and finished with his blessing. As the entity left, there was a loud growling sound and the room seemed to shake. Then everything was still. Emily fell into a sound, untroubled sleep and, according to her parents, hardly got up for the next two days straight.

Grant and I got Annie to give us her Ouija board, and we removed it from the house. We've remained in contact with the Sawyer family, and we know that the demonic activity that plagued their family has ceased. The exorcism worked.

At T.A.P.S., we get "possession" calls all the time. Ninety-nine percent of them turn out to be bogus. This one was all too real.

GRANT'S TAKE

When we experiment with the occult, we're not just endangering ourselves—we're endangering those around us. We can say all we want that we're not our brothers' keepers. But when it comes to the supernatural, we *are.*

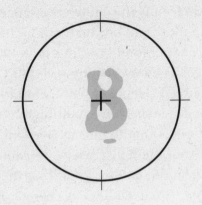

SQUEAKY TOYS
SEPTEMBER 1998

Usually, dogs and cats react to spirits in a negative way. It's difficult to say why. Maybe they're sensitive to the paranormal in ways most human beings aren't. But in the ghost-hunting field we never say never, because we're constantly coming across exceptions to the rules.

One of them was in Toms River, New Jersey, in the condominium home Jim Coors shared with his dog Benny. We knew that the condo had been a flour mill at one time, so we kept that in mind during the investigation.

The problem, as reported by Coors, was that his dog liked to play with squeaky toys and the sounds of these toys kept him up at night. As a result, he had taken to stowing Benny's three toys in a closet outside his bedroom. This seemed like a logical measure—until one day, Jim woke to the sound of squeaking and found Benny playing with his toys.

Thinking the closet door might not have locked, he went to check it out, only to find that it was closed. A curious situation, to say the least. The next night, Jim put Benny's toys away in the closet again—and found them in Benny's possession the following morning. As before, the closet door was shut, and Coors couldn't imagine how Benny had gotten the toys.

Still trying to puzzle it out, he took his regular morning shower. As always, his bathroom mirror steamed up. There was nothing unusual about that. But when he got out of the shower, he saw handprints in the steam—small ones, like a child might have made. Freaking out a little, Coors tried to wipe off the prints, but they wouldn't go away . . . because they were on the *inside* of the mirror.

After that, Coors noticed his dog playing with something he couldn't see. This began to happen on a regular basis, making Coors wonder what was going on. But it didn't actually scare him until he saw Benny playing with what appeared to be a small boy. A single man without any children, Coors went over to investigate and saw the boy dissipate like smoke on the wind.

It wasn't the last time he would see the boy, either. The child turned up on Jim's stairs, walking down them as if headed for the living room. Again, as soon as Coors approached him, he vanished.

And the squeaky toy problem kept getting bigger. The more Coors tried to keep the toys from Benny, the more they multiplied. New toys showed up alongside the old ones, though Coors hadn't bought them. By the end of

October, he found himself shoving as many as twenty toys into the closet at night. By the next morning they were out again—and the closet door was still locked.

At his wits' end, he called in T.A.P.S. Grant and I showed up with Keith Johnson, Heather Drolet, and our usual complement of recording equipment. Heather was a single mom with three kids, who also happened to be a practicing pagan. When she first joined the group, we put her in charge of personnel, but she wanted to do more.

As we started bringing her along on investigations, we discovered that she was an uncanny interviewer. She could be as nice as you please but get just about anything out of anybody. She would ask a question five different ways until she finally got a reasonable answer.

In this case, however, we wanted her to learn more about the equipment, so while Grant and I interviewed Coors and calmed him down, Heather and Keith walked through the home and set up our instruments. Then we began our investigation.

The whole time, Benny looked at us with his big, innocent eyes. If he knew the truth of the situation, he wasn't telling. One thing was for sure, though: he wasn't skittish. If there was a spirit in the house, it didn't bother him in the least.

The first thing I did was kick the shower on full blast at its highest temperature. When the room steamed up, it bore out what Coors had been saying. There were child-sized handprints on the inside of the mirror, and they wouldn't go away no matter how much I wiped at them.

Unfortunately, we didn't pick up any other evidence of the paranormal that night. But those handprints were clear proof that something was going on in the condo. Packing up and taking a couple of squeaky toys with us for analysis, we embarked on the research phase of our investigation.

It turned up some interesting information. Apparently, a ten-year-old boy had died of pneumonia in the immediate area, and the child Coors had seen playing with Benny looked to be about that age. We wondered if the boy's spirit was the presence Coors had been experiencing.

As I mentioned, animals are usually stressed out by the paranormal. But if Benny was only seeing a small boy, he might not have felt threatened, regarding the boy as a playmate.

The one aspect of the case we couldn't explain was the proliferation of squeaky toys. However, we offered the homeowner Keith's services as a priest if he wanted to cleanse his condo of its resident spirit.

As it happened, Coors wouldn't have any part of it. Now that he knew he was dealing with a child-entity and an apparently benign one, he felt much more comfortable with the situation. Even the squeaky toys didn't seem to bother him so much—but he did give up on locking them up at night.

GRANT'S TAKE

People often get weirded out by supernatural activity. It's only normal to fear what we don't understand. But when our clients see what they're dealing with, they sometimes—like Jim Coors—choose to embrace it rather than chase it away.

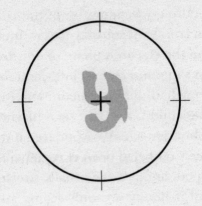

INCUBUS
JULY 1999

Everyone in Rhoda Long's historic Newport, Rhode Island, neighborhood thought she was crazy when she said she had been violated by an invisible entity.

At first, she had only seen shadows that shouldn't have been there and heard noises she couldn't explain. Then, in the middle of the night, she woke to the sound of growling and a feeling that someone or something was holding her down. At the same time, she felt a terrible pressure between her legs, an insistent pushing that she desperately wanted to stop.

But she couldn't. In fact, she couldn't move at all. She could barely even breathe, the air was so thick and heavy around her.

The feeling lasted for only twenty seconds, but it felt

like a lifetime. When it finally ended, Rhoda sat up in bed and gasped for air. Her husband, Roger, alarmed by her behavior, asked her what was wrong. When she told him, he didn't know what to make of it. Eventually, they went back to sleep and tried to forget about it.

Unfortunately, it wasn't Rhoda's last such experience. A few days later, she was coming out of the shower when she got the feeling she was being groped. Again, it only lasted for about twenty seconds. But this time, she was left with more than a memory. She had red marks all over her torso—the kind a pair of grabbing hands might have made.

Needless to say, Rhoda was scared out of her wits. And it got worse that night, when she felt pressure again in the same place, and again she couldn't move to try to make it stop. It was as if she was paralyzed, if only for a few seconds.

Rhoda told people what had happened to her, but no one seemed to believe her. She became a nervous wreck, dreading the idea of falling asleep. She began chain-smoking cigarettes, though she had seldom smoked them before.

And the violations kept occurring.

After a while, the nightmare expanded to other parts of Rhoda's life. She would leave her kitchen in perfect order and come back to find all the cabinets open. At least once a day, she heard banging sounds coming from her basement.

Finally, she called in T.A.P.S. Hearing how troubled she was, Grant and I put together a team and responded as quickly as we could. Because of the nature of Rhoda's experiences, we brought along a woman team member, Heather Drolet.

When we arrived, Heather sat down with Rhoda to interview her and reassure her while the rest of us explored the house. Heather found that Rhoda had occasionally used a Ouija board, which can give demonic spirits an excuse to enter a house. It wasn't a good sign.

In the meantime, Grant and I checked out the basement, where Rhoda had heard banging sounds. Being plumbers, we were able to come up with an explanation for the noises. The city of Newport has notoriously high water tables, and the Longs were running a sump pump to keep water from flooding their basement. However, the pipes in the basement weren't braced, so when the water table rose and the pump came on, the pipes would bang. Nothing supernatural there.

But the banging had been the least of Rhoda's problems. As we continued our investigation, I entered the Longs' bedroom and lay down to get the feel of the place. Before long, I felt a weight on my chest—exactly what Rhoda had described. When I tried to get up, I couldn't.

It wasn't a pleasant sensation. And as I lay there, I thought I saw someone leave the room. But at that point, my fellow ghost hunters were elsewhere. I should have been all by myself.

A few seconds later, the feeling passed and I was able to get up. But I'll never forgot the feeling of helplessness I experienced. I began to get an inkling of what Rhoda was going through.

Grant and I talked about it and admitted the possibility that Rhoda was being tormented by an incubus—a demonic spirit that lies down on sleepers, especially women, in order to have sexual intercourse with them. The incubus is also said to drain energy from its victim in order to sustain itself.

On the other hand, there was a scientific explanation for her troubles—a phenomenon called sleep paralysis. Sufferers find they can't move, get the feeling that someone is on top of them, and sometimes see shadowy figures. But I had felt the same thing in the Longs' bedroom, and I had never been prone to sleep paralysis before.

In the end, we weren't able to document Rhoda's experiences. However, in light of what had happened to me and the intensity of Rhoda's feelings, we had Keith Johnson perform an exorcism. We stayed in touch with the Longs after that, but they never again reported any experiences out of the ordinary.

Most of the time when we run into a paranormal entity, it's a benign one. If there was an entity plaguing Rhoda Long, it was what we call "negative" or "inhuman." That's the kind we don't play around with.

GRANT'S TAKE

One of the reasons people reach out to us is a need for assurance that they're not insane. Rhoda Long's experiences were horrible enough without her having to doubt her sanity. Fortunately, we were able to help her on all counts. In our field, that's a home run.

WHAT A CHILD SEES
AUGUST 1999

When an adult reports the sighting of a spirit, all kinds of questions arise. When the reporter is a child, and a very young one at that, there are even more questions—from her parents in particular. Is their child crazy? What should they do to make the sightings stop?

Four-year-old Selena Taylor told her parents, Louis and Delia, that she talked to "Grandma" on a regular basis. Unfortunately, her grandmother had passed away several months earlier. Louis and Delia might have chalked this up to their child's imagination except for the fact that Selena seemed to know things only her grandmother could have told her.

Beyond that, objects were disappearing in the Taylor house, a single-family duplex in Franklin, Massachusetts.

There were noises at night and sometimes during the day. And both adults in the house reported catching glimpses of a human-looking figure.

When T.A.P.S. arrived at the Taylor residence, at about four o'clock on a sticky summer afternoon, both the Taylors and their daughter were present. While the rest of the team went around the house and looked for places to set up equipment, Keith and I interviewed the adults, who told us about the entity they believed might be the ghost of Louis's mother.

The entity hadn't given any indication of being hostile or aggressive. The reason the Taylors contacted us was that they wanted to make sure that they—and their daughter, especially—weren't in any danger.

Next, we interviewed little Selena. She sat in her big red chair and refused to talk to us until we played a while with her beany animals. Only then did she start to open up to us. We found her to be very articulate, and not at all afraid of what was happening to her. But then, she was still young enough to believe in Santa Claus and the Easter Bunny, so to her anything must have seemed possible.

By six o'clock, we had two camcorders with infrared capability running upstairs, one in the girl's bedroom and one in her parents' bedroom. According to the Taylors, the entity had appeared in both places. If it existed, there was a good chance we would catch it on videotape.

Nothing happened until a quarter to eight, when Selena informed us that she had seen her grandmother while walking upstairs to her room. The entity had walked past her into one of the house's two spare bedrooms. Changing tack, we redeployed our equipment. In a matter of minutes, we had installed infrared cameras and motion sensors in the bedroom the girl had indicated.

About half an hour later, the motion sensors went off. Rushing up to the room to see what had happened, we checked the infrared cameras. Unfortunately, there was no visual evidence of anything.

At 9:30, Selena was put to bed. But by 10:00, she was back downstairs to tell us that her grandmother had spoken to her and said she wasn't in the house to harm anyone—only to watch over the family. We asked Selena why her grandmother hadn't passed over to the other side. She said her grandmother just wasn't ready.

The Taylors were comforted by this information. They told us that if the entity was in fact their grandmother, they didn't want to push her out. They just wanted us to gather evidence and document her activity.

At 11:15, the motion sensors went off again. This time, the infrared cameras captured some apparent orbs, but nothing more. At midnight, we heard someone moving about in the kitchen, though neither the Taylors nor any member of our team was supposed to be in there. When we checked, the kitchen was empty.

Grant and I asked the Taylors if they would like us to bring in a clairvoyant, or a sensitive, to try to communicate with the entity. The Taylors liked this idea and gave us the go-ahead. By 5:00, we hadn't picked up anything else, so we packed up and left—with the understanding that we would be back.

Five days later, we returned with the same team that

had worked on the case previously, as well as Bethany Aculade, the sensitive who had worked with our group in the past. Bethany met with the family, discussing the things she would say to the entity and also what she would not say.

The Taylors stressed to Bethany, as they had to us, that if the entity was Louis's mother, they didn't want to make it leave. Bethany acknowledged that wish and began preparing for a communication with the entity in Selena's room, where it had been seen most often.

At 9:00 p.m., there were seven of us in the girl's bedroom: the three Taylors, Bethany, Grant, Keith, and me. Bethany started trying to communicate with the entity by means of clacking—the tapping together of two sacred stones in an attempt to speak with the dead. It has been said that the energy from the impact and the resultant noise helps the spirit to communicate and sometimes even show itself.

Almost immediately, the temperature in the room dropped. This was especially surprising considering there were seven people in a 12-by-15-foot enclosure, and common sense would tell you it would get warmer in there. Bethany interpreted the temperature change as the spirit's way of trying to communicate with us.

Selena confirmed it: her grandmother was in the room with us. Our EMF meters were showing marked fluctuations in the room's magnetic field, adding credence to the idea there was a supernatural presence among us.

We watched as the little girl carried on one end of what seemed to be a two-way conversation. Every so often, she relayed a message to one of her parents or a member of our

T.A.P.S. team. However, we had no hard-and-fast evidence that she was in contact with her grandmother—only her word for it.

Abruptly, Selena stood up and asked, "Are you sure?" We didn't hear an answer. Without warning, the girl walked out of the room.

Curious, we all followed her. She led us downstairs, all the way to the basement, where we watched her dig through some cardboard boxes at the back north end of the room.

None of us knew what she was doing. We just stood there, looking at each other.

Finally, Selena pulled out a small wooden box, turned to look past us, and asked, "Is this the box, Grandma?"

She must have received a reply in the affirmative, because she said, "Okay," and opened the box. There were pictures inside—old ones, from the look of them. And something else.

A diamond ring.

Handing it to her mother, Selena said, "Grandma wants her ring."

It was one of the eeriest moments I have ever experienced. And though one question seemed to have been answered, it gave rise to another one. If Selena's grandmother had indeed requested her ring, how were we to get it to her?

Sitting around the Taylors' kitchen table, we talked about it. The family decided that they would go to the deceased woman's gravesite in the morning, dig a hole over her coffin, and put the ring in it.

A week later, we contacted the Taylors to find out how things were going. They told us that they had indeed buried the ring and that the spirit's appearances in the house had ceased.

We are still in contact with this family, and they haven't had a single paranormal experience since.

GRANT'S TAKE

Sometimes people have no idea whose spirit may be haunting them. In this case, the Taylors had an idea of that long before we got there. Our job was only to confirm it—and help them figure out what to do about it.

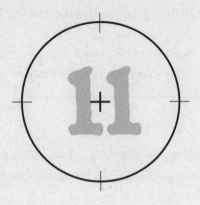

UNFINISHED BUSINESS
SEPTEMBER 1999

More often than not, the paranormal events we encounter are the results of tragedies that occurred a long time ago. But in some cases the tragedies are much more recent, and it requires some sensitivity on our parts if we're to conduct an investigation.

In this particular instance, we were called down to southern Connecticut to help a well-to-do couple plagued by a number of odd events. Vases had toppled over and broken without explanation. Necklaces and other valuables had gone missing, only to be found later in another part of the house. The wife, whom we'll call Lisa Edison to ensure her privacy, had been awakened by voices in her bedroom. Both she and her husband, whom we'll call Robert, had seen fleeting apparitions throughout their home.

Also, the stereo in their daughter's room had been discovered blasting in the middle of the night. This was especially disturbing because their daughter, Jennifer, had been killed in a drunk driving accident on her way to school on graduation day. Her parents kept her ashes on the mantel in the living room.

Because the family couldn't deal with a full-scale investigative team, Grant and I approached this case on our own. As soon as we spoke to Lisa and Robert, we could tell that Jennifer had meant everything to them, almost to the point where they couldn't live without her.

Grant spent a lot of time with Robert, listening sympathetically to how much the man missed his daughter. I used that time to talk to Lisa. She showed me Jennifer's diary, which she had found after her daughter's death. It said that Jennifer had been miserable, that she had been closer to her friends than her family, and it spoke of how she would escape to the beach whenever she could. That was when she was happiest—when she was sitting in the sand, surrounded by her best buddies.

We interviewed both Lisa and Robert pretty extensively, all the while being careful not to add to their pain. Then we walked around the house with a camera, an EMF detector, and an audio recorder. Unfortunately, we didn't experience any activity.

The next day, Grant and I went over the recording of our interview with Lisa and Robert, hoping it would give us an idea as to how to continue our investigation. What we heard knocked us off our seats. In addition to the voices of Lisa and Robert, there was a third voice—one that was distinctly female. As we listened to it, we heard the names Joe, Aaron, and Melissa.

Returning to the Edison house, we played the interview for them and asked them if the names were familiar to them. Lisa said they were Jennifer's closest friends, though Lisa wasn't very fond of them. At our suggestion, she agreed to invite the three kids over the next day.

Joe, Aaron, and Melissa all showed up, but they were obviously pretty weirded out. Unlike Jennifer's parents, they didn't want to get to the bottom of what was happening. They just wanted to put their friend's death behind them and move on.

As we talked with the three of them, we found out a couple of things. First, the song that Lisa had heard blasting from Jennifer's stereo had been their theme song as friends. Second, Jennifer and her friends had all made a pact: when their time came, they wanted to be buried somewhere near the ocean.

Grant and I suggested the idea of having a ceremony on the beach and casting Jennifer's remains into the water. Her parents were reluctant to do that, however. After all, this was their only child and her ashes were all they had left of her. It was certainly understandable.

But later, when Grant and I played back the interview with Jennifer's friends, we heard a female voice again. This time it said, "Water," and "Get out." When we told the Edisons about this, they relented.

Sometime later, they had a ceremony on the beach and entrusted their daughter's ashes to the waves. They experienced no more activity from that point on.

GRANT'S TAKE

Spirits are limited in the ways they can communicate with the living. They can't always tell us outright what they need or want. But if we open ourselves up and listen closely enough, we can hear them.

GHOST LOT
NOVEMBER 1999

A few years after we started T.A.P.S., a woman named Maura, who lived not far from Grant in western Rhode Island, told him that her grand-parents were hearing and seeing strange things in their two-bedroom home.

What kind of things? Unearthly growls from somewhere inside the house. The sound of gravel crunching in the driveway outside. Doors opening and closing on their own. Blurs and shadows in almost every photograph taken in the house. Every so often, Maura's grandmother, Helen, saw a scraggly-looking figure standing outside her bathroom or in the backyard.

But the most unsettling incident was one that involved the family cat, which had gone missing. When they found it, its torso had been ripped away, leaving only its exposed spine to hold its upper and lower halves together. You can imagine how upset they were.

Grant and I checked out the house on our own. It was a good thing he knew the area, or I might never have found the place. It was dark out, and the area was too rural to have streetlights. When we got close, I could see that the house was built on a hill, with a gravel driveway curling around beneath it.

Maura and her grandparents were nice people. That much was obvious. They were also troubled by all the goings-on. You could see it in their eyes.

We all sat for a while in the living room, talking about what had happened and how we were going to proceed that night. Then we set up our equipment and went to work. For the rest of the evening, we heard what sounded like footsteps, but we didn't hear growls or see any apparitions.

Then, around 12:30 in the morning, we heard the crunch of gravel outside the house and the thud of horses' hooves. Shooting to our feet, Grant and I peered out into the darkness from the family's enclosed porch. The sound of hooves had abated, but we heard the scrape of boots and people talking.

Without our coats, we went outside to see what was going on. But when we got out there, there was nothing to see. No horses, no people, and no explanation for what we had heard. We went back inside.

For a while after that, it was quiet both inside and outside the house. We listened for a repeat of what we had heard before, but there wasn't any. After a while, we wondered if that was all we would get that night.

Then we heard three amazingly loud growls from under

the dining room table, which was only about six feet away from us. After we caught our breath, we agreed that the sound had come from a particular spot in the floor. Examining it, we found loose floorboards. With some trepidation, Helen told us it would be all right to pull them up.

When we did, we found a trapdoor.

Grant and I exchanged glances. We knew the answer to all the house's troubles might be down there under that door. Preparing ourselves for what we might find, we swung it open. Underneath there was a hole of some kind, choked solid with rocks. They had some kind of markings scratched into them, but we had no idea what they meant.

While Grant was looking at the rocks, I happened to glance in the direction of the bathroom—and saw a tall, shadowy man dressed in scraggly clothes standing there and watching us. By the time I pointed him out to the others, he had gone back down the hallway. We pursued him, but we couldn't find any sign of him.

Helen hadn't seen the apparition this time, but she agreed that the description I gave her was the figure she had seen before. She seemed relieved that I had caught a glimpse of it too.

As it turned out, we weren't done hearing sounds that night. But the ones we heard next weren't at all like the others. They sounded like someone pounding the underside of the floor. When we checked it out, we found evidence of a leaky pipe.

Now, we may be ghost hunters when we're investigating claims of the paranormal, but we're also plumbers. When we see a leaky water line, we can't just ignore it. We have to fix it.

In this case, that was easier said than done. The only practical way for us to address the problem was to lay in a new ten-foot piece of copper pipe and solder it into place, and we only had a small, unlit crawl space in which to work. What's more, there was hand-blown insulation above and below. If we hit the insulation above us with the flame from our torch, the house would go up like a Roman candle. If we hit the insulation below us, *we* would go up.

So we had to be extra careful. First, as we made our way through the crawl space elbow over elbow, we sprayed down the insulation with our water bottles. Then we laid a foot-square fire blanket under the section we would be soldering, so we wouldn't drip any molten metal on anything flammable. It was a tough job, but we had come to help—one way or the other.

By the time we were done, it was almost dawn. We packed up our stuff, told Helen we would be in touch with her, and headed back home. But we were eager to see what we had picked up on our equipment.

When we ran our analysis the next day, we saw that our cameras hadn't recorded anything interesting. It was a pity. We were hoping to have gotten some footage of the scraggly figure near the bathroom.

However, when we went over our audio footage, it was a different story. To our satisfaction, we had captured some EVPs. *Nasty* ones.

The first had been recorded when those three loud growls had come from under the dining room table. As it turned out, there were nine growls altogether, three before the ones we had heard and three more immediately after.

The second EVP came up when we found the trapdoor and saw the man in dirty clothes watching us. As he retreated into the hallway, we heard a voice saying something like, "Now, now, now, dirty folk . . . mean."

Of course, the job wouldn't be done until we had conducted our research. Grant and I spent the next couple of days poring over records and visiting the local historical society. Finally, we struck pay dirt.

The house had been built in the middle of a "ghost lot"—an area marked on old maps to denote a territory held sacred by its original Native American inhabitants. Such places are thought to be haunted by Indian spirits. Not a good place to build, you would think.

And yet, someone had—a man named Jeremiah, who had owned not only the ground on which the house was built but also any number of acres around it. Apparently, the entities that haunted his land, which he'd referred to as "dirty folk," had driven him crazy enough to burn his house down.

The police had responded to the blaze in horse-drawn carriages, and they'd taken Jeremiah away. In the end, he'd accomplished only part of his purpose. He'd burned down the house, all right, but its foundation had been preserved. It was on this foundation that Maura's grandparents' house had been constructed.

Armed with this knowledge, the couple made the decision to have the entity removed by their clergyman.

GRANT'S TAKE

We were probably a little crazy to try to lay that copper pipe in that little crawl space. One wrong move and we would have been ghosts ourselves. But our business is helping people, and we do that any way we can.

GOOD SPIRITS AND BAD
DECEMBER 1999

People have all kinds of personalities and disposi-
tions, good and bad. So, apparently, do ghosts.
And sometimes, you get both kinds at once.

Pia and John Devine lived in a two-bedroom bungalow
in a suburban community in central Rhode Island. The first
inkling they had that something was amiss was when their
two-year-old son, Jack, woke up screaming in the room he
shared with his younger brother Joshua. When Pia went
into the room to see what was the matter, the hysterical Jack
pointed to his rocking chair.

It was empty, but Jack kept pointing to it as if there had
been someone sitting in it. Pia did her best to soothe her
son, then she put him back to bed.

She was still pondering the incident the next day when
she caught a glimpse of a strange figure in her kitchen—a

woman wearing white. It shook her up. And soon after that, she felt a male presence in her basement and a female presence elsewhere in the house.

She didn't know where to turn. Eventually, she heard about T.A.P.S. and gave us a call. Four of us—Grant, Keith Johnson, Andrew Graham, and I—visited her house to see what we could find.

By then, the Devines had experienced other disturbing phenomena. Pia had heard a female voice singing lullabies in her children's room. John had felt an uncomfortable presence in the master bedroom late at night. And Pia had discovered what sounded to us like ectoplasm on the children's unused changing table.

She had inadvertently captured yet another phenomenon. Pia, who was an accomplished violin player, had recorded herself playing one day. When she played back the recording, she could hear faint voices calling her name.

T.A.P.S. wound up spending two weekends collecting evidence at the Devine house. We found what appeared to be three distinct supernatural entities. One, a female, was clearly interested in the children. A second seemed to wish only to be left alone in the basement. The third, a spiteful spirit, seemed intent on agitating the entire Devine family, as well as the female spirit.

While we were conducting our investigation, both Jack and Joshua were in hysterics, and neither of them would go to sleep. However, they were fine once they left their bedroom. At one point, Pia went into the children's room and came out petrified. When Grant and I went to see what disturbed her, we found that the room was five degrees warmer and the air was difficult to breathe.

We addressed what we believed was the mischievous entity, and the room went pitch black. The air seemed to become even thicker, and the temperature shot up another sixteen degrees. We couldn't speak for a moment, it was so oppressive in there.

Finally, we were able to find the words to call Keith, who blessed the room. After the blessing, the children seemed to have no trouble going to sleep. However, to rid the Devines of the mischievous entity, we would have to bless the entire house.

In the end, Pia and John decided to remove the spirit that was tormenting their children while letting the two benign spirits remain. We had no problem with that. To date, the unfriendly spirit hasn't come back, and the Devines are enjoying their other two guests.

GRANT'S TAKE

During our stay with the family, it seemed to us that Pia was becoming sensitive to supernatural phenomena. Having had our own experiences with sensitivity, Jason and I advised her as to how to deal with it. We were able to give her some perspective on what could have been a very troubling time in her life.

THE PERSECUTED HUSBAND
MAY 2000

Like living people, ghosts have their own agendas. Some people fit into them and others don't. And if you're one of those who don't, they can make your life a hell on earth—as they did for one poor guy in eastern Connecticut.

In this case, a haunted house situation, we were brought in by Maine Paranormal Research, a member of our T.A.P.S. extended family. Four of us went to check it out—Grant, myself, Keith Johnson, and Shelley King. Shelley, who was an early member of T.A.P.S., specialized in finding EVPs, or electronic voice phenomena.

What we found when we arrived was a two-level home with two bedrooms, a large walk-in closet, a bathroom, a kitchen, a dining room, an attic, and an unfinished basement. Nothing out of the ordinary—or so it seemed.

The couple that lived there had an unusual relationship in that neither the husband nor the wife was home much of the time. Then again, they didn't have any kids—just a big, friendly mastiff. Erica, the wife, worked for a hotel company and traveled a lot to other countries, while Frank, her husband, worked for a construction company in Florida building high-rises eight months out of the year.

Frank was a tough guy by all appearances and professed not to believe in ghosts, but he was clearly starting to get paranoid. He related one instance to us: he had been standing on a table in his barn when he felt something shove him, causing him to lose his footing and go crashing to the ground. On another occasion, he'd been standing in the house's main hallway when he felt something push him from behind.

But those hadn't been his only bad experiences. Doors that had politely remained open for his wife had closed on him when he walked by. He had woken up sometimes in the middle of the night to see something standing over his bed—often enough that he had taken to sleeping downstairs on the couch.

Interestingly, Erica wasn't plagued by any of this activity. What's more, female friends would say they felt extraordinarily comfortable in the house, while men who visited felt nervous and distinctly unwelcome.

For reasons she couldn't identify, Erica felt that she knew the spirit's name. She called it Michael.

Once the interview was over, we began setting up our equipment—camcorders, high eights, and digital recorders—pretty much wherever Frank had experienced activity. Unfortunately, we didn't have any luck at first. No EVPs, nothing on video, no personal experiences.

Then Grant, who was going upstairs to the attic, felt something grab his leg. Naturally, he thought it was me. I do that to him sometimes when I'm kidding around. Suspecting that I had done it in this case as well, Grant turned to sock me in the arm—but no one was there.

He finally found me two stories below, talking with Erica and Frank, and gave me the shot he had been saving up. "You grabbed my leg," he told me when he saw the puzzled look on my face. "I did not," I said. And the homeowners backed me up. Grant still thought I was pulling a fast one, so he checked the camera in the room where we were standing. Sure enough, I had been down there for some time.

Something else had grabbed him.

Encouraged by Grant's experience, we continued to seek out evidence of the entity Frank had described. Hours went by, but as before, we were stymied—until we went into the second bedroom, the only room in the house with no reported activity.

No sooner had we opened the door than we saw a shadowy mass in the corner of the room. It wasn't shaped like a man. In fact, it wasn't shaped like anything. It was like a heat mirage, the kind you see coming off a hot summer sidewalk in the distance. Except that it was pitch black.

Approaching it, Grant and I reached into it and felt an almost Arctic cold. It seemed to us there was electricity in there as well, though not enough to give me any serious kind of shock. Then the mass disappeared.

But it wasn't gone completely. A moment later, one of us spotted it in the bathroom a few feet away. Again Grant and I tried to touch it, and again we felt a terrible cold, like the inside of a meat locker. This time when it vanished, it returned to the bedroom where we had seen it originally. When we followed, it went past us like a stiff wind—and wasn't seen again the rest of the night.

In the wee hours of the morning, we packed up and headed home. The next day, we went over the footage we had taken. Unfortunately, we hadn't managed to get the black mass on videotape. However, we had captured some rather interesting EVPs.

One of them said, "Get out now." Another said, "Leave here." And a third, recorded when the entity had left the second bedroom like a harsh wind, said, "Get down from there. You're wasting your time." The words were whisper-thin but unmistakable.

We also did some research on Frank and Erica's house, which turned up a nugget of interesting information. A man named Michael had indeed been a previous resident of the place, but not recently. He had lived in the house a couple of centuries earlier. Michael's wife had cheated on him with another man, causing him to murder her in a fit of jealous rage. The man with whom she had cheated had then killed Michael, completing the circle of tragedy.

If the supernatural entity in the house was Michael, it was no wonder he didn't like seeing men there. Of course, he might have been hostile to women too, considering what his wife had done, but he seemed to have a soft spot for them.

We offered Erica Keith's services as an exorcist, figuring she would want to get rid of the spirit. But she said she wouldn't mind hanging onto it. After all, the spirit offered her comfort while her husband was away down in Florida.

Which left Frank in a difficult spot. His wife had gotten

attached to a paranormal entity, and as far as we could tell the feeling was mutual. We suggested that Frank cut a deal with the spirit: he would leave it alone if it left him alone.

Frank felt funny about the idea, but he couldn't live with what was going on. In the end, he agreed to talk with the spirit. Soon after, the hostile incidents stopped, and to this day the spirit seems to be abiding by the deal.

GRANT'S TAKE

It was a strange triangle that developed in Erica and Frank's house—a man, a woman, and a ghost. I'm not sure I could have lived with it, if it had been me. But it kept Frank from getting hurt, so who are we to judge?

THREE WIVES
OCTOBER 2000

Sometimes we feel so victimized by supernatural entities in our homes that we forget who the real victims are. That was what happened in the western Rhode Island home of Becky Jones, an elderly woman who called T.A.P.S. out of pure desperation.

While rummaging through her attic, Becky had seen three apparitions at the same time. Frightened to her marrow, she'd gotten out of there as quickly as she was able, and she'd resolved not to go up again. But she seemed to have awakened something.

The next day, when she'd entered the large old barn in her backyard, she'd felt the place start to shake. There had been no wind to speak of and nothing hitting the barn from the outside, but it had shuddered as if the earth were quaking beneath it. Again, she'd had to escape as quickly as she was able.

Afterward, her dog had taken to barking loudly and urinating at the entrances to the attic and the barn. And at night, she'd heard crazed laughter from the attic, as if someone had been up there. Finally, she hadn't been able to stand it anymore, and she'd reached out to us.

Usually, we're right on time for our investigations. This time traffic held us up, and we arrived later at Becky's house than we had intended. As we hurriedly worked to unload our car, wanting to get set up before dark, I happened to glance at the small, round window in the attic. There were faces up there, watching us. Heather saw them too. I grabbed a camera and snapped a picture of them.

But when we went up to the attic, there was no one there. Going back downstairs, we saw that the faces were gone, and we resumed unloading our car. Once we were done, Keith and Heather sat down to talk with Becky, while Grant took a video camera out to the barn. I followed him out there a moment later.

I was still thinking about the faces as I entered the barn, so I wasn't prepared for the incredibly loud growl I heard or the force that pushed me back out again. A moment later, Grant emerged and told me he had been inside and he'd heard the growl. It had been all around him, like thunder. The barn had shaken so hard that he'd fallen to his knees.

In the house, Keith, Heather, and Becky could hear screams coming from the attic. They called us in to tell us about it, and we told them about what had happened in the barn. We also said we weren't going to let it stop us.

As we entered the barn a second time, there wasn't any

growling or shaking, but I felt a pressure in the air that made me extremely uncomfortable. Grant had the same feeling. Nonetheless, we stayed long enough to set up a couple of cameras.

Then we did the same thing in the attic and went back downstairs. For a couple of hours, we waited for the growls and the screaming to resume, but nothing happened. You would never have known there had been such a racket in there earlier.

While Grant and Heather stayed in the kitchen to hold Becky's hand, Keith and I went up to the attic to check on our camera. We found that the battery was dead, though it had been fully charged when we left home. Since we didn't have a spare, we packed up the camera—at which point our flashlight went dead as well, plunging us into darkness.

We could feel a presence with us in the darkened attic. It was unmistakable. Then I heard the whispered words, "Martin, want out!" They sent chills up and down my spine. Descending from the attic, I asked Keith if he had heard the voice. He said he had.

In the morning, we left Becky but assured her that we would be back as soon as we could analyze our data. When we went over our video footage, we caught a few moments of a form approaching the camera in the barn. Also, our still picture of the attic window revealed some shapes, if not actual faces, that shouldn't have been there.

Obviously, something had happened in either the barn or the attic or both. We just didn't know what. It wasn't until we researched the property that we began to get some answers. We learned that the man who'd built the house had mysteriously lost not one but three *wives*. Then he'd gone insane and killed himself in the barn.

Though we had no real proof, we surmised that he had locked his wives in the attic one by one until they'd starved to death. Then—and again, this was supposition—they'd haunted him until he'd gone mad and taken his own life. In any case, these spirits weren't going to be easy to make a deal with.

Our only real recourse was an exorcism, which Keith was happy to perform. Afterward, the house became quiet again, much to Becky's relief.

GRANT'S TAKE

I had never before experienced anything like what happened in Becky Jones's barn. It was worse than an earthquake, from what I've heard about them. It was more like being in the eye of an incredibly loud and tumultuous storm—and not knowing if you were going to survive.

INTRUDER
NOVEMBER 2000

When T.A.P.S. embarks on an investigation, we look for natural explanations before we entertain the possibility of supernatural ones. We try to debunk claims of ghostly entities and occurrences. That sets us apart from other ghost-hunting groups, who go in with the preconceived notion that a place is haunted.

Don't get me wrong—I believe in the supernatural. I think there are ghosts all around us. I just don't think ghost hunters are going to advance our store of knowledge, or our credibility with the public, if we label everything a haunting.

We explain our position to our clients in advance. After all, eighty percent of the time we have to tell them they've got a loose floorboard and not a spirit of the dead. Usually that's enough to put their minds at ease, and we feel good that we were able to help.

When Deena Jackson asked us to investigate her Uxbridge, Massachusetts, town house, we responded immediately. After all, Deena had a six-year-old daughter, and we don't like to see children hurt or victimized by fear. When we arrived, Grant and I sat down and spoke with Deena while Keith Johnson and Heather Drolet did a walk-through and set up equipment.

Deena complained of several problems. For one thing, she felt she was constantly being watched. For another, she heard a banging in the walls at all hours. She also heard footsteps at night, though there was no one there to make them. Finally, her downstairs television appeared to turn itself on at night.

It appeared to Deena that her home was haunted. She was concerned for the safety of herself and her little girl. It was an understandable reaction.

In our exploration of the town house, in Deena's bedroom closet we came across several books on ghosts and hauntings. Sometimes that's an indication that the client is trying to fake a supernatural event, but we didn't believe that was true in this case. Deena seemed genuinely scared by what was happening.

The first claim we checked out was the sound of footsteps late at night. Deena's neighbor walked his dog at night. It was possible that what she'd heard were his footsteps on the staircase outside.

We trained a camera on the downstairs television, hoping it would turn on and give us some evidence. We also checked on it from time to time. However, it remained inactive the entire night.

Deena had also spoken of a banging sound in the walls.

We didn't have to wait long to hear it. However, it sounded like her neighbor's headboard hitting the wall between his town house and Deena's.

Of course, not everyone who lives in a town house hears what goes on in her neighbor's home. But these homes were rather new and had walls built with metal two-by-four studs. This allowed sound to travel easily and efficiently from one residence to another.

After a while, we called it a night. When we came back to Deena with our analysis, we had to tell her that we didn't think her home was haunted. After all, we hadn't been able to document any of her claims. In addition, none of us felt anything out of the ordinary there. It seemed like a secure place to raise a child.

Deena rejected our findings out of hand. Despite everything, she was certain that her home was haunted, and she wouldn't hear anything to the contrary. It wasn't our job to convince her one way or the other. All we could do was tell her what we had seen and wish her good luck.

GRANT'S TAKE

We're not mean people. We would rather have a happy client than an unhappy one. However, we've got to call 'em the way we see 'em, and the way we saw Deena Jackson's house was "not haunted."

THE HAUNTED WAREHOUSE
FEBRUARY 2001

We've all heard of haunted houses, but how many of us have heard of a haunted warehouse? We at T.A.P.S. have not only heard of such a thing but we once had the opportunity to investigate one.

The warehouse in question was located in central New Jersey. It was an old building, though we were unable to determine how old, or what it was used for originally. All we knew was that it was big—80,000 square feet of storage space spread out over three floors.

We were invited there by Sam Dillon, the warehouse's manager. He and other employees had experienced what they could only describe as supernatural occurrences, though he was the only employee there when we arrived. As we set up our equipment, we asked him to tell us exactly what had happened.

On one occasion, Dillon said, he and two other employees were ascending the south staircase, talking about work, when they all felt they were being pushed from behind. On another occasion, he and another employee saw a man in a tan work shirt who glanced at them and then appeared to walk through a wall.

Shortly thereafter, an employee was having trouble pushing a heavy cart up a ramp. Finally, he decided to take a break before giving it another shot. When he returned to the cart, he saw it was at the top of the ramp—and a pitchfork had been stuck in one of the wooden steps that ran along the ramp's flank.

At first, the employee thought that some of his coworkers had done the job for him as a joke. But they said they hadn't. They also claimed they didn't know where the pitchfork had come from.

After that, the incidents became more widespread. Employees began seeing nebulous masses in the warehouse. Some said they were black, some said they were gray, and some said they were red, but almost everyone encountered one of them.

The building alarm began going off every Wednesday, regardless of how many times Dillon had the system serviced. Employees were calling in sick and quitting. It got to the point where people were scared to enter the building.

After we finished interviewing Dillon, he took us up to the third floor, which had no windows. It was almost perfectly dark up there, but we were all able to make out moving shapes. As we got closer to them, they seemed to disappear.

Later that night, Andrew was pushed from behind and

nearly fell down a flight of stairs. At the same time, we recorded some EVPs—though we wouldn't hear them until the next day, when we analyzed our data. They were voices telling us to "Leave . . . leave, gather."

At a few minutes after 3:00, we all suddenly smelled food and heard what sounded like many voices coming from one end of the warehouse. Dillon told us that the smell and the sounds were coming from what used to be the building's cafeteria.

Later, while we were investigating the second floor, we heard the sounds of footsteps and sliding objects coming from the floor above us. Keith and I also witnessed several orange lights whipping through the building. We tried to come up with an explanation for them but couldn't.

Finally, we decided we had seen—and heard—enough. We packed up and assured Dillon that we would be in touch with him. Then we headed back to Rhode Island, eager to go over our footage.

Our analysis documented the EVPs, if not a whole lot else. However, when we combined the data with our personal experiences in the warehouse, it was difficult not to concede that there was something supernatural afoot.

Unfortunately, we were unable to piece together who was haunting the premises and why. It was an old building and probably had an interesting past, though none of it was documented by the historical societies in the area. We would have loved to spend more time there but were unable to do so.

One story that Dillon told us may have accounted for some of the paranormal activity. According to one story, the building used to have a security guard who would travel up and down the stairs during his rounds, pushing people out of his way. If that's so, his ghost may still be doing so.

We suggested to Dillon that Keith bless the building and try to exorcise the spirits in it. Dillon agreed, and the procedure was carried out. We have since heard that some activity has been noted, but Dillon is of the opinion that it is simply people's imagination and nothing to be concerned about.

GRANT'S TAKE

I have to admit that I was skeptical when I heard about the pitchfork. That just seemed like the product of an overactive imagination. But after experiencing what went on in that warehouse, I'm more inclined to believe the story.

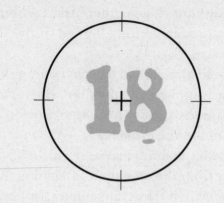

GHOSTS WITHOUT LEGS
APRIL 2002

One of our strangest cases took place in a New York City suburb, where two children were being scared to death by apparitions without legs. They were so distraught that they were actually poking their eyes to keep from seeing the things.

Normally, Grant and I like to stay home with our families on Christmas Eve, just like anyone else. But when we heard what these children were going through, we knew we had to put our holiday aside. Keith Johnson and Heather Drolet must have felt the same way, because they agreed to go with us.

When we arrived, Heather and I interviewed the homeowners, Amy and Gary Stanton, while Grant and Keith began setting up our equipment. We learned that Mindy Stanton, age seven, had seen a human figure move through her bedroom without noticing her. And for some strange reason, the figure seemed to be buried in the floor up to its hips.

Twelve-year-old Marcus had seen an entity walking in the hallways, similarly sunken into the floor. He too said the entity hadn't appeared to notice him. Alan, age fifteen, hadn't seen anything out of the ordinary.

But Mr. and Mrs. Stanton had seen a male figure walking down the stairs from the second-floor landing, its feet buried in the steps. When they confronted it, it had vanished. All three apparitions had recurred in the same locations.

We explored the entire house and recorded both video and audio for several hours. Unfortunately, we didn't get any results. When we left in the early hours of the morning, we had nothing to offer the family.

However, our research turned up some interesting information. Apparently, the house was built on what used to be farmland, and the farmer's house, which had been torn down long ago to make way for a suburban development, had stood on more or less the same spot. It occurred to us that the apparitions were the occupants of the farmhouse, tied to the place for reasons we couldn't begin to imagine.

But why would they appear to be sunken into the floor? Because the floors of the farmhouse had been lower than the floors in the Stanton house. The apparitions were still walking in the paths they had always walked, unaware that a second house had replaced their own.

From all indications, this was a residual haunting—one that plays itself over and over again, like a broken record. The supernatural entity can't interact with its environment. It's just a pattern of energy left over from its earlier activities.

We offered the family our theory. But even if it was accurate, they were too scared to let the situation continue. In the end, they had the house blessed, which reportedly eradicated the entities from their home.

GRANT'S TAKE

Those legless apparitions had to be a frightening sight. In some cases, knowing what's causing the haunting makes it less chilling for the observer. But not in this case.

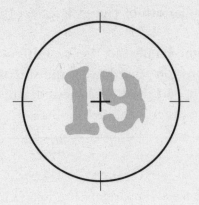

THE BET
JULY 2004

The best result we ever got from an investigation was at Race Rock Lighthouse on the west end of Fishers Island, a vicious-looking pile of rock that sits at the eastern entrance to the Long Island Sound. We were invited there by the Coast Guard, which had been frustrated in its attempts to prove or disprove rumors that the place was haunted.

Race Rock had certainly seen its share of tragedies over the years. During the early 1800s, vessels struck the partially submerged formation with shocking regularity. The best-known ship to wreck itself on the reef was the steamer *Atlantic,* which went down in the autumn of 1846. Forty-five people perished that day.

Finally, the government decided to erect a lighthouse on the rocks. One of the engineers who worked on the project,

Francis Hopkinson Smith, also built the foundation for the Statue of Liberty in New York Harbor. It took seven years and great courage on the parts of dozens of workers before Race Rock Lighthouse was completed in 1878.

For years, the rocks were manned by a succession of hardy lighthouse keepers. But after a while a solar cell was installed, and the lighthouse no longer needed a human being to run it. Today the Coast Guard makes periodic maintenance visits, but no one lives there.

Unless you believe the stories about the lighthouse keeper's ghost. Then you would have to amend that statement.

Six of us from T.A.P.S. were slated to hook up with the Coast Guard in New London, Connecticut, and get a ride to the lighthouse. Because the place is no longer furnished, we had asked Brian to pick up some folding chairs at my house. As far as I knew, he had that job covered.

Unbeknownst to either Grant or myself, Brian had forgotten the chairs. "He'll frickin' kill me," he muttered, referring to *me*. And I would have. It wasn't as if we could just scoot on back to the mainland whenever we felt like it. Once we set up on Race Rock, we would be stuck there for the night.

Fortunately Andy Andrews, a new investigator in the group, had backed Brian up and packed the chairs. Brian was relieved, to say the least. If I had known the chairs were missing, I would have been on his case all night.

We had also brought along Heather Drolet. Heather was an expert in the use of divining rods—a pair of metal sticks that can detect ambient energy. Since ghosts draw on the energy around them in order to manifest themselves, Heather's talents seemed likely to come in handy.

When the Coast Guard arrived, we met Senior Chief Boatswain's Mates Jennings, Osborne, and Nolda. Having heard the stories about the lighthouse keeper for so long, they were looking forward to the investigation. So were we, even though we would have to cover eight miles of choppy seas before we got to Race Rock.

When we came in sight of the place, we realized why so many ships had run aground there. Two strong, savage currents were clashing at the rock, churning the water around it into a giant whirlpool. It was crazy.

There was no way any of us could have made it to the dock. However, the Coast Guard guys made it look easy. We worked harder than usual unpacking our equipment, considering we had to hand it up from a rocking boat instead of simply carrying it out of a truck. Also, we had to bring our own generator, since there wasn't any power available to us in the lighthouse.

All in all, it promised to be the most difficult investigation we had ever undertaken. Not only were we dependent on our generator for power but we also had to be careful not to slip on the rocks and end up in the drink. Worst of all, the lighthouse didn't have a single bathroom that still worked.

Fortunately, we were all used to improvising.

One of the Coast Guard's claims was that they had heard the shower going one time they visited the lighthouse. Of course, when they went to check it out, it was turned off. To observe the shower, we trained a couple of cameras on it and set up an EMF detector, which measures energy fluctuations. Then we put others in the basement, where the spirit of the lighthouse keeper had been known to appear.

One thing you need to know about me is that I have a playful side. Even in the middle of the most serious investigation, I might grab Grant's leg or play a prank. I was in that kind of mood at the lighthouse.

In fact, I had felt like that all day—which was why I had brought a fishing rod along with all our other equipment. While the rest of the team investigated the insides of the lighthouse, I was going to spend the night fishing.

It wasn't as crazy as it sounded. Ghosts have been known to manifest themselves outside as well as inside. In a place like Race Rock, it wasn't a bad idea to have a set of eyes on the rocks themselves.

Just to make it interesting, I got ahold of Brian and wagered two hundred dollars that I would catch a fish that night before he caught a ghost. Being the earnest soul he is, Brian took me up on the bet. I didn't know what the fishing would be like, but I didn't get a real haunted feeling from the lighthouse, so I thought my money would be safe.

As Brian investigated the place, he offered to cut a deal with the lighthouse keeper's ghost: if he let Brian obtain proof of his existence, Brian would split the two hundred dollars with him. It made sense in a bizarre sort of way, though I can't imagine what the ghost would have done with the money.

In the meantime, Grant made his way up to the attic and sat down in one of the chairs we had brought. We do that sometimes—just sit in a place, soaking up the atmosphere. But he couldn't stay up there long. It was just too warm.

At this point in the investigation, Heather and Andy were working together, Heather using her divining rods and Andy using an EMF detector. We wanted to see how the two modalities compared to each other. As luck would have it, neither of them came across anything significant.

Out on the rocks, I wasn't having any better luck than they were. I had been out there for hours already without a bite. At least I had some company in the form of one of the Coast Guard guys—Chris Osborne, or Oz, as he liked to be called.

We were talking about fishing, about ghost hunting, and about the Coast Guard. Just passing the time. Then I asked a question about something, I don't remember what. But I do remember Oz not answering.

His eyes had narrowed, as if he was trying to concentrate on something behind me. I turned around, but I didn't see anything. Just big, fat billows of fog.

"What is it?" I asked.

"There's someone out there," he said, already on his way back up to the lighthouse. "I just saw a flare."

It seemed unlikely that anyone would be cruising around in that fog. But if they were, they were in terrible danger. The rocks were dangerous enough even on a clear night. On a night like this one . . .

As it turned out, there *was* a boat out there. By the time the Coast Guard guys got to it, it had smashed against the rocks and was taking on water pretty quickly. As I watched from shore, the Coast Guard brought in the boat's crew.

Two guys, a father and son. The dad was maybe fifty, the son half of that. They had been out there for hours, their motor having conked out. The flare Oz had seen had been their last one. And the dad was a diabetic. He was already starting to have problems, so we got him inside the lighthouse and gave him orange juice and fruit.

The two of them were extremely, extremely fortunate. The fog, the rocks, and the waves made for a deadly combination. If we hadn't chosen that night to conduct our investigation, they would probably have drowned.

Funny how things work out.

Anyway, neither Brian nor I won our wager. He didn't find any ghosts, and I didn't catch any fish. When morning came, we packed up our stuff and headed back to the mainland. Needless to say we were disappointed, but the Coast Guard guys were even more so.

Of course, we still had to analyze the data. When we did, we found some interesting things. A tendril of fog, for instance, that made its way into the bathroom and got thicker in the vicinity of the shower. And a cluster of orb activity, though neither Grant nor I are big on those phenomena as reliable indicators of the supernatural.

However, the real eye-opener took place in the attic. We saw Grant sitting in the chair and opening himself up to the vibes in the place. Then we saw him get up and leave the room. As far as we knew, that was the end of it.

But as soon as he was gone, the chair slid across the floor.

It was dark in the attic, and we were concerned that we might have misinterpreted what we had seen, so we sent the tape out to a videographer of Andy's acquaintance. The guy cleaned up the tape and sent it back. It was just as we had thought. The chair had slid across the floor of its own volition.

"So something happened," I conceded, despite my earlier feelings that the lighthouse was free of ghosts. My colleagues weren't satisfied. "All right," I said, "the place is haunted."

But the best thing we caught that night was that boat with the two guys in it. After all, our mission is to help people. You just never know whom you're going to help.

GRANT'S TAKE

No one was more surprised than I was to see that chair move. One minute I was sitting in it, all unsuspecting, and as soon as I was gone it slid across the floor. It gives me chills just thinking about it.

THE CAPTIVE DEAD
SEPTEMBER 2004

There aren't many venues like Eastern State Penitentiary anymore—a gray stone fortress in the northwest portion of Philadelphia, Pennsylvania, that would have put some medieval castles to shame. The place was shut down years ago, when it became too expensive to run. But according to stories, some of the prisoners remain—at least in spirit.

Grant and I had been hoping to investigate Eastern State for some time, so you can imagine how excited we were when the invitation came. But no one was more excited than Steve and Brian, who had heard the tales circling the penitentiary like vultures and were eager to see what it offered. It would be interesting. Both of them were stimulated by even the slightest sign of supernatural activity, though Steve was always levelheaded in the end.

If Grant and I were ever to place T.A.P.S. into anyone else's hands for a hiatus, Steve would be our man. He would take care of the organization just the way we do, and it would be in the same condition when we returned.

We put together a team of six for the haul down to Philadelphia. It included, in addition to Brian and Steve, Carl Johnson and Sheri Toczko. Sheri, whom Steve had brought into the group, had never been on a ghost hunt before, but she had always been interested in the paranormal. This was her chance to see it up close.

Before we arrive, T.A.P.S. researches every place we investigate, but we still weren't prepared for Eastern State's immense size. When we drove up, the prison's caretakers invited us to park our vans right there on the grounds behind the iron gates. Then they gave us an extensive tour of the place. Because it's such a unique and impressive venue, a brief history is in order.

It all started with the Quakers. They pretty much ruled the Commonwealth of Pennsylvania during the 1800s, and they had an idea that it would be better if prisons served as places of spiritual reform rather than mere holding cells. Influenced by Enlightenment thinking and visionary physicians like Benjamin Rush, they believed that people who committed serious crimes ought to be isolated so they could spend time in contemplation and penitence.

Eastern State was built over a period of ten years and opened for business in 1829 while still under construction. It was one of the most expensive buildings erected to that point in time, with its thick, medieval-looking walls, its vaulted windows, its arched corridors, and its imposing guard towers. From a central hub called The Rotunda, seven long, stony cellblocks radiated like the spokes of a wheel. The place became an architectural wonder that attracted international visitors and encouraged imitation.

Each prisoner had a room with a toilet, running water, and a skylight dubbed the "Eye of God." They were allowed contact with only a guard or a minister—no one else. When taken from their cells, prisoners were hooded so they wouldn't be distracted from the business of humility and spiritual transformation. Supposedly, with nothing else to do but contemplate his crime, a prisoner would learn to so hate it that he would never again be tempted to do such a thing. Charles Dickens, on the other hand, viewed these methods as an ignorant "tampering with the mysteries of the brain," which were potentially worse than torturing the body.

There were any number of "inducements" for a prisoner to pursue remorse and repentance. He might be confined in a straitjacket, given an ice-cold bath, entombed in a vermin-infested trench, thrown into a much smaller cell than his own, strapped overnight to a wall, or belted into the "mad chair"—a device intended for uncontrollable psychotic patients. Worse, he might get the Iron Gag, where the convict's hands were crossed over his chest and tied, while a device was locked over his tongue that would torture him as he moved.

Eventually these practices subsided and the place became a bit more humane. The prisoners were allowed to mingle, develop skills in workshops, communicate with the outside world, and even form teams for sports like baseball and football. Still, they always had to return to their cold, dark cells.

Among the more notorious inmates at Eastern State was gangster Al Capone, who was sentenced in May 1929 to a year's confinement as a punishment for carrying concealed weapons. But he wasn't uncomfortable there. He was allowed to furnish his cell with a rug, an antique desk, a lamp, a radio, oil paintings, and an easy chair to make his stay there more pleasant. Today's tourists get to see the place decked out the way Capone had it, and the contrast between his cell and the others is startling. He was even allowed to make long-distance telephone calls and conduct business from the warden's office.

Nevertheless, isolation got to him (as it did many others), for he began to complain of a ghostly visitor—one of the men who had been gunned down in the St. Valentine's Day Massacre. It's probably worth revisiting that bloody chapter in the history of organized crime to understand who might have been haunting Capone, and why.

On the morning of February 14, 1929, seven men were standing in a red brick warehouse on Chicago's North Side, waiting for a delivery from the S-M-C Cartage Company. This was during Prohibition, when the government clamped down on booze, but these gentlemen weren't exactly the most law-abiding citizens. They were awaiting a truckload of bootleg whiskey that would be distributed to illegal pubs, called speakeasies, around the city.

Instead of the truck, a police car pulled up to the building. Three men wearing police uniforms and two dressed as civilians got out of the car and went inside the warehouse. It looked like the authorities had caught on to the illegal delivery.

But a few moments later, residents of the neighborhood

heard the rattle of several machine guns. After the occupants of the police car piled back inside and took off, a few brave souls entered the warehouse. They found a horrific scene: the seven men lay on the floor, each one shot in the back multiple times. The wall against which they had been lined up for the assassination was a gory mess of spattered blood and bits of human flesh.

Obviously, the shooters had only impersonated officers of the law. It was in actuality a gangster hit. Since the victims were known associates of mobster George "Bugs" Moran, Moran pointed the finger at his rival, Al Capone, who was in Florida at the time. Naturally, Capone pointed back at him.

The truth didn't come out until investigators were finally able to match a bullet to a machine gun found in the home of one of Capone's hit men. Moran was right. Capone's men had lured the victims to the warehouse and then slaughtered them.

One of these victims, James Clark, had been Bugs Moran's brother-in-law. After Capone moved into Eastern State, the other inmates could hear him screaming at night for "Jimmy" to leave him alone. Having heard the details of the crime, they assumed that the ghost was Clark. Capone apparently continued to be haunted by this spirit even after his release, because his bodyguards later reported that they would hear him begging "Jimmy" to depart.

Capone's valet supposedly saw this apparition for himself on one occasion. Capone believed that the spirit had followed him from Eastern State, although why it would have decided to appear to him there is anyone's guess. Perhaps the conditions were just right.

Like any place that's been around a long time, the prison went through waves of renovation over the years. They included the 1956 addition of a death row, with its own exercise yard for some of the country's most dangerous men, which remained in use until 1972.

It is estimated that upwards of 80,000 inmates were processed through Eastern State over the years. Some of them never got out. The prison now sits empty and crumbling, a National Historic Landmark open for tours, art exhibits, and a special monthlong Halloween extravaganza.

It was an interesting venue for an investigation, no question about it—especially since Capone's story wasn't the only one worth checking out. After all, plenty of inmates went insane in this building. Many others died, either from abuse, old age, illness, or at the hands of other inmates.

Staff members who work late have reported eerie sensations, the sound of footsteps in cells or corridors, strange laughter, and glimpses of fleeting things in the shape of humans. Often they were seen darting into a cell. Of considerable interest to us were the staff's reports of a dark figure in cellblock 12 that walks the long, dank corridors or just stands still, always reeking of malevolence. Another phantom figure is sometimes spotted in the guard tower, as if one conscientious guard just can't leave his post. A number of people who work on the ongoing restoration feel they're being watched by someone.

We couldn't wait to unload our equipment and get set up. The question was where to focus our resources. The place was too big for us to cover in a single night.

I didn't know what to make of Capone's experience, since that could have been his own mind playing tricks on him. Since he wasn't around any longer, there was no way to re-create it. However, the other prison stories we had heard suggested that we had both residual and intelligent hauntings on our hands.

A residual haunting is the most common variety. It's as if some person or event left an impression in time the way a seal leaves its image in hot wax. The entity, when seen, may seem to be lost in a time warp. Often it seems mindless and confused or unaware. That's because it's not actually there, but energy from the person or event lingers nevertheless.

In these types of hauntings, people may hear screaming, crying, footsteps, or a name being called out. They even smell perfume, or the odor of cigars or pipes. We don't know exactly why residual hauntings take place, but we believe that they start with a violent event, like a murder, or the loss of a loved one. This creates an energy that replays itself over and over in the same place, either on an anniversary or more regularly.

One thing to remember about residual hauntings is that they pose no danger to the observer. The entities aren't aware that anyone is watching them. They just go about their business.

An intelligent haunting, on the other hand, is the result of entities that are aware of their surroundings and can freely move around. So you might see an entity in cellblock 12 that then shows up in a guard tower. That makes our decision as to where to place our cameras more uncertain. You just don't know where entities will be, although they tend to at least stay in the same building. Sometimes they can move objects, and often they will see the living and try to communicate.

They want to be noticed, and they can do things that scare the living, particularly because—like a flashlight—they do their most noticeable work during the darkest hours of the night. They can be benign or mischievous, perhaps wanting to drive people away or wanting to deliver some piece of information that will finish their business on this side. Maybe they can't accept the fact that they've died, or they're trying to watch over someone. Whatever their reason for being there, they don't want to leave.

We decided to set up our four remote cameras in two places—cellblock 4 and cellblock 12—because they had the highest volume of reported activity. Our command center would be in The Rotunda. At any given moment, at least one member of the team would be there to catch anything the rest of us missed.

Grant and I had to remind everyone that this wasn't a Halloween tour. We were professionals. It was hard to resist being influenced by the cold, dank setting, with its crumbling walls, rows of empty cells, and dark corridors, but we had to go about our investigation as we always did—with an eye to objectivity.

Carl Johnson went off to leave a voice recorder in one of the cells where he sensed a presence might be trying to communicate, while Brian and Dave Hobbs, one of our cameramen, approached cellblock 4 to collect EMF readings. An electromagnetic field meter shows different types of spikes for different types of energy. We believe that a certain range of spikes indicates the presence of an anomaly in the electromagnetic field.

Grant and I were watching Brian and Dave from the monitor station when suddenly they gave a shout, wheeled, and came running the length of the cellblock back to The Rotunda. This really annoyed me, but I waited until they arrived, out of breath and wide-eyed, to hear their explanation first. They looked like they had seen a ghost—maybe several.

"Dave had just taken a picture," Brian explained, huffing and panting, "when a black shape went right across in front of us. It went right across my face. I saw shoulders and a head. Dave freaked and ran, and then I freaked and ran." For some reason he thought that what he was saying would excuse his behavior.

"You ran like a sissy," I admonished him. "You can't do that on an investigation."

Brian didn't have a good answer for that. Instead of responding, he turned around and walked away. It was a good thing. Angry as I was, I might have said something we would both have regretted.

Grant and I checked out the cellblock. After all, we wanted to see if there was really something there. But we couldn't find anything.

"The flash must have screwed up their eyes for a second," I ventured.

"Still," said Grant, "you've got to walk out calmly. It's unprofessional. The people who work here saw that."

What if we had been in somebody's house? The last thing you want to do as an investigator of the paranormal is panic the people you're trying to help. True, we never know what we're going to encounter, but we're supposed to be documenting our experiences, not fleeing from them.

Brian eventually acknowledged that we were right. He was torn between the delight of a little kid who had gotten what he was hoping for and the calm manner of an investigator who wants to be taken seriously. For us, he had to be the latter. There was no compromise—even if the devil himself had crossed Brian's path in cellblock 4.

By 4:00, we found ourselves wishing we had more time there. It was such a fascinating place, and we had barely scratched its surface. But morning was coming and we had to wrap up.

Back at our headquarters in Warwick, Rhode Island, Steve and Brian set about analyzing our data. They found only one anomaly, but it was an interesting one. In cellblock 12, where people had reportedly seen a dark entity either standing or darting around, our camera had picked up a mysterious image.

It was a little vague, but it looked like someone in a dark robe approaching the camera and then turning to go back the way it came. When we measured it against the rail next to it, the figure couldn't have been more than four feet tall—an unlikely height. We ran the footage again and again, wishing we could see it a little more clearly.

Was it possible that someone had pulled a hoax on us? We always had to ask ourselves that question. But our team was eating at the time, and so were the penitentiary people who had stayed with us overnight. And as far as we knew, there wasn't anyone else around.

We kept running the image again and again, but we could not make it out any better. So we sent it out to a professional lab to have it lightened up. If we had something, we wanted to get the best image we could.

I also made a point of congratulating Brian for finding the image. He and Steve had spent hours and hours poring through uneventful footage to pick out that one brief but promising morsel. I wanted him to know I appreciated it and that I took note of the good work he did as well as the bad.

But even if we got a great look at the figure, it wouldn't be enough. T.A.P.S.' reputation was on the line here. Before we conceded that the image was evidence of a haunting, we had to do everything in our power to debunk the notion.

That meant going back to Philadelphia. And this time, we wanted to have two full nights to run a thorough investigation.

In other words, two more nights away from home and work—two more nights we would have to explain to our wives. But when we told Kris and Reanna that it was a matter of credibility for T.A.P.S., they understood. In fact, they found it kind of exciting that we might have gotten such a dramatic image. Go figure.

So we drove down to Philadelphia again and set up the equipment the way we'd had it before, but we added a new item. In cellblock 12 this time, Grant and I walked side by side down the pitch-black corridor with a thermal-imaging camera, which picks up variations in temperature and offers a more discerning image than infrared.

We also brought along more help in the form of former police officer Brian Bell, a tech-savvy guy who had been helping us with various applications back at headquarters. He had expressed a desire to go out on investigations, so we were giving him an opportunity to do so.

Bell's job the first night would be to man our split-screen monitor station in The Rotunda. If anything came up, he was to tell us.

Grant and I went directly to cellblock 12, where our infrared camera had picked up the image of the cloaked figure. We checked out the structures overhead to see if someone might have been up on the third level using lights to create the image we had captured. Grant even went so far as to climb up there. But after trying every angle, we decided the idea wasn't plausible.

We also scanned the cellblock with our thermal camera. Almost immediately, we saw something dart by across the mouth of the corridor, but it was only a cat. A little later, we picked up a bright spot that seemed like it might be something interesting. Unfortunately, it was nothing more than a reflection.

At the same time, Steve, Brian Harnois, and Sheri were checking out death row, also known as cellblock 15. Finding a vaporous anomaly that showed up on their still pictures, they followed it around. After taking a half-dozen photos of it, they lost it and decided to return to The Rotunda.

Grant and I had the same idea. But when we got back to The Rotunda, we found Bell's chair empty. He had disappeared somewhere. Now this really annoyed me. Whoever was watching the cameras had a responsibility to the team. No matter how many hours he might have to spend staring at the same image, there was a reason for it. Something important might appear at any moment—and last only a second. We had counted on Bell to do this job.

I asked around, and it turned out that he'd gone across the street to a gym, supposedly to wash his hands. I was steamed.

"You assigned him," I told my partner.

Grant nodded. He knew what I was getting at. He hates

doing this kind of thing, because he just wants everyone to do their jobs, but he agreed that he'd have to have words with Bell. And he knew it would go down better if he did it instead of me, considering the mood I was in. People who must leave their posts are supposed to find substitutes so the monitors don't go unattended. It was just one more un-professional act by a T.A.P.S. member at this investigation, so I was aggravated.

It was tough for Grant to address the problem, but he told Bell in no uncertain terms that we had to be able to count on him. He was not to leave his post for any reason without someone covering it. We thought he understood, but truthfully, we had no way of knowing.

Before we knew it, we were pushing daylight. It was time to wrap up. Securing our equipment, we went back to our hotel for a few hours' shut-eye.

At nine o'clock, we gathered for breakfast downstairs. We had plans to make for the second night of our investi-gation, and we wanted everyone to be present as we made them. Everyone was on time . . . with one exception.

Brian Bell.

After waiting for half an hour, Grant and I went up to his room and knocked on his door. When he answered it, I said, "Good morning, Sunshine."

Grant had another talk with him. He told Bell that he kept dropping the ball. "We can't count on you," he said.

I was less than optimistic that Bell would come around. In a very short time, he had established a track record, and not a good one.

Anyway, we all had breakfast, made our plans, and showed up again at Eastern State. A little after nine o'clock, we got the enhanced video footage back from the lab. We all gathered in The Rotunda, eager to take a look at it.

Unfortunately, the processing had only lightened the image a bit. The figure was still difficult to make out. I felt we needed more of a perspective on the situation.

Then I got an idea. I asked Brian Harnois to pull a blanket over his shoulders so it would look like a cloak, then position himself in cellblock 12 where our camera had recorded the mysterious figure, and run forward and back again. In this way, he would be simulating what we had seen on the videotape.

Brian complained that he couldn't see, so he couldn't run. Still, he did his best to cooperate. Then we compared the results with what we had in the can, but nothing in Brian's performance even came close to replicating the image we had recorded. For one thing, he was much taller than the ghostly figure, as we had expected.

Just after two in the morning, we all got together again in The Rotunda. All of us except . . . you guessed it. Brian Bell was nowhere to be found. He wouldn't even answer his cell phone. Obviously, he had a lot to learn about teamwork, let alone ghost hunting.

(Not long after this investigation, we let Bell go. He was just too much trouble, too high-maintenance.)

Grant and I took one last look at cellblock 12 with our thermal-imaging camera. But it wasn't a thermal image that grabbed us. It was a feeling of heaviness—the same one in two different places—as if we were walking through a cloud. Grant even went so far as to say he was having trouble moving his feet.

We also saw things. Grant caught a glimpse of a shadow

in the space above us. I saw one slip out of a cell and disappear. Those experiences alone were worth the trouble of returning to the penitentiary.

We logged it all and added it to the data we had accumulated. It was about 3:30 a.m. That's the time, worldwide, when the most paranormal activity is reported.

When we got back to Warwick, Steve and Brian Harnois took a couple of days to go over everything. In the end, all they had to show for it were the stills they had taken on death row—the ones that showed the vaporous anomaly moving about the corridor. However, we had four separate personal experiences to go by, not to mention the footage of what we had come to believe was an apparition.

We decided to put the footage on our website. We wanted to see if other people were as impressed with it as we were.

Our final report to the people who ran the penitentiary was that we believed the building was haunted. What's more, we had had so much fun there that we wanted to visit the place again in the future.

GRANT'S TAKE

I t takes some work to find people who live up to what they say they can do. Lots of people are eager to go on a ghost-hunting jaunt, and they assure us they're serious, but the tedium of the long hours deep into the night puts them to the test—and not everyone passes. Only a few will stick with us, investigation after investigation, and those are the ones we come to trust the most.

The thing about voluntary groups is that some people interpret "voluntary" to mean it's not as serious. To us it's very serious. We're driven by the desire to know what the paranormal is all about, and we rely on a team of responsible people who understand the agenda and will do their part to support us.

TOPTON HOUSE
SEPTEMBER 2004

The smell of roses. In a storage cellar.

That was a new one on us. However, that was one of the claims made by Francine Gore, owner of the Topton House restaurant in Topton, Pennsylvania. Whenever one of her daughters went down into the cellar, she smelled roses.

Gore also claimed that a mischievous entity, the spirit of a little girl who had died of pneumonia in the building back in 1870, was haunting the non-smoking dining room. It got its kicks by tripping the restaurant's patrons, who were then puzzled as to what had tripped them. If someone left a soda on top of the bar, the girl spirit would move it out of reach.

People had also seen a woman in a light blue dress with her hair wrapped up in a bun. She would stroll past the doorway, enjoying the place like any living patron. But when someone pursued her, she disappeared.

Built in 1859, the Topton House was originally used as a restaurant and inn by people using the nearby railroad line. During the Prohibition era it was a speakeasy, an illegal public house. One of the beams in the basement is charred from a fire many years ago—more than likely the result of an illegal still.

We were brought to the investigation by Rick Bugera, president of the Berks Lehigh Paranormal Association, a T.A.P.S. family member. Rick and his group had conducted an investigation of Topton House on their own, with inconclusive results. He wanted to see if we could find anything definitive.

Even if we did find evidence of the supernatural, Gore didn't want the spirits evicted. She wanted them to remain part of the ambiance of the place. She told us about a customer who had walked into the restaurant, announced that there were twelve spirits in evidence there—which, apparently, was too many—and walked out again. However, most patrons seemed to find the possibility of ghostly presences charming.

For this investigation, Grant and I had brought along a bigger group than usual—not only Brian, Steve, Andy, and Keith but also Amy Andrews and Sheri Toczko. Amy was a Reiki master, Reiki being the art of healing through energy manipulation that had sensitized me to the paranormal when I was younger. Of course, most people don't have the reaction I did.

We had included Amy because we knew she would bring a different perspective to the investigation. Sheri was a novice who wanted to learn more about ghost hunting. She was also fast becoming Steve's girlfriend.

That was fine for Steve and Sheri, but it was a problem for T.A.P.S. It's difficult enough to remain focused throughout an all-night investigation. When your love interest is sitting right next to you, you're too likely to miss the three-second phenomenon that might make the trip worthwhile.

To be honest, we hoped the relationship would fizzle out before it went too far. If it didn't, we were going to have to talk with Steve and Sheri. Life is full of choices. We just hoped they would make the right ones.

The easiest claim to check out was the one about the glass of soda. We put a glass full of Coke on the bar and trained a camera on it. If it moved any time during the investigation, we would know it.

The smell of roses in the cellar was a little trickier. However, when we went down into the cellar, we saw a hole lined with leaves that gave access to the outside. Obviously, a smell or combination of smells might have made their way through the hole into the basement.

On the other hand, there weren't any rosebushes near the hole. There were some in front of the restaurant and in the florist shop across the street, but those places were too far away to be of consequence. So why would we concern ourselves with the hole?

The answer lies in the concept of matrixing, in which the mind creates sensory impressions when it tries to interpret certain stimuli. Sometimes somebody smells a campfire when there's nothing around but bug spray and lemon meringue pie. We believed that kind of thing was happening in the cellar of the Topton House.

It was Grant who came up with the idea of testing the possibility that the smell might be coming from outside by taking a bottle of cologne and spraying it in the garden. The Gore daughter who had smelled the roses joined us in the cellar for our experiment. When Grant sprayed his cologne, we could smell it in the cellar—no doubt about it. Now, the smell of cologne is stronger than the smell of roses, I'll grant you. But even a faint smell can be detectable if it's manufactured over the course of days or even weeks.

Francine's middle daughter told us she was sensitive to supernatural occurrences, and that she had experienced something in the cellar as well. On Friday nights, she was sometimes called on to bring up a case of beer for the bartender. She wouldn't even get halfway down the stairs before she got the feeling she was being watched. As soon as she went back up the stairs, the feeling would be gone.

We sent Steve, Brian, Sheri, and Amy down to the cellar with the girl in the hope that she would attract the spirits she usually attracted. Unfortunately, they got mixed results. Every time the girl felt something, it would disappear—as if the spirits in question didn't want to be detected.

Brian suggested that they break a rule we have in T.A.P.S. and split up to examine different rooms in the cellar. In this case, it was excusable. No one was going to be more than ten feet away from the next person. Still, they didn't find any evidence of the supernatural.

Having broken one rule, Brian decided to break another one. He asked the young girl to come down the stairs the way she usually did—this time with an audio recorder in her hand—and see if she got the same feeling. "Are you a happy spirit?" she asked as she descended. "Why are you here? Are you afraid of something? Are you afraid of me?"

Nothing much happened. However, we had another audio recording to go over when we got home. That might prove to be valuable.

While we were there, we asked Amy to perform Reiki on the middle daughter, as a way of testing her claim that she was sensitive to the spirit world. Amy observed that the girl had great energy in her. And afterward, Amy said she felt calmer and lighter for the experience.

When we checked on the glass of Coke, we saw that it hadn't moved. Having covered pretty much all the ground we had hoped to cover, we called it a wrap. Thanking Francine Gore and her daughters, we headed home.

Brian and Steve conducted our analysis back in Warwick. They found a weird shadow on the wall, which could have been the result of an internal adjustment in our infrared camera. Unfortunately, that was it.

We believed that we had debunked the smell-of-roses incidents, and we couldn't come up with documentation of any of the other claims at Topton House. So while we couldn't say the place wasn't haunted, we hadn't found any evidence to say that it *was*. All that remained was to apprise Francine Gore of our findings.

We wondered how she would receive them. Not well, we expected. Grant is better at handling delicate situations, so we decided that he should be the one to speak with her.

Discussing our findings with clients—what we call the "reveal" stage of an investigation—is sometimes a problem for us. After all, most ghost hunters "find" ghosts wherever they go. We, on the other hand, end up debunking eighty percent of the cases in which we get involved. In other words, eight out of ten times we have to tell our clients their place probably isn't haunted.

In some instances, people are relieved to hear that. More often, they're disappointed, because they want some validation of their experiences. They don't want to have to consider the possibility that they're crazy, or at least misguided.

In cases like Topton House, there's an economic consideration as well. Hotels and restaurants can often bring in more business if there's credible evidence of a haunting there. And the people who own these places are almost always people we would like to help out.

But we can't base our results on whom we would like to help, or how we would like to help them. We find what we find, and we report accordingly. Which is what we did when we met again with Francine Gore.

As we predicted, she wasn't pleased, and she expressed her disappointment that we hadn't found anything. However, she was every bit the lady we'd hoped she would be. We were able to leave feeling good about our investigation, which is really all we can ever ask for.

Incidentally, Sheri didn't stay with us too much longer. She was a sweetheart, but she had an interest in graphic arts that she wanted to pursue. Steve still keeps up a relationship with her, but only as a friend.

GRANT'S TAKE

Why am I the one who's always got to give people the bad news? Because, of the two of us, I'm the one with all the patience. Or so my partner keeps telling me.

THE ARMORY
OCTOBER 2004

Like people, ghosts have their own rules. Abide by them and they may leave you alone. Break them and you may wish you hadn't.

The Armory in New Bedford, Massachusetts, had seen its share of guilt, despondency, and despair. Built in 1903, it had welcomed soldiers home from a half-dozen wars, each man carrying his unique backpack full of horrors. One might have been suffering from post-traumatic stress disorder, one might have discovered that his wife had been cheating on him, and one might have felt he just didn't fit into society anymore. Every soldier's story was different, yet they were also very much the same.

Too often, the burden proved to be more than the guy could carry, and he sought relief the only way he could. In the office, a first sergeant hanged himself from the ceiling.

Another poor soul hanged himself in a back room. Yet another guy was depressed because he was separating from his wife, so he went into his office and blew his brains out.

The most famous story involved a general who was really rough with his troops. The thing he hated the most was horseplay. If a soldier played a prank, the general would discipline him hard. Apparently, he was hard on himself as well, because he committed suicide one night on the armory drill floor.

It wasn't surprising that guardsmen had reported paranormal experiences over the years. Guys had seen footsteps appear in puddles of water. They had gotten shoved by unseen entities. In the hallways they had heard and seen figures that disappeared under close scrutiny.

T.A.P.S. was invited to investigate the place by the local National Guard battalion, the idea being to prove or disprove the stories once and for all. Our team of five was shown around the armory by Sgt. Joe Rebello, the battalion's medical section chief. In addition to the usual core group of Steve, Brian, Grant, and me, we had along Mike Dion, a seasoned investigator from the T.A.P.S. group in Massachusetts.

Rebello had had some experiences of his own, which he described to us. One night when he was alone, he heard a door slam on its own. When he looked into it, he couldn't figure out how it had happened. On another occasion, a hot night in August, he suddenly felt cold and his breath froze right in front of him. In fact, cold spots turned up in the building all the time.

We were eager to begin our investigation. However, since we had arrived earlier than usual, we took a lunch break first. None of us blinked when Frank DeAngelis, our sound technician, tripped one of our cameramen. It was the kind of practical joke we play on one another all the time.

But Rebello and Sgt. Steve Thrasher, another armory officer, seemed to cringe. When I asked why, they reminded me about the general who hated horseplay. Apparently, his spirit wasn't tolerant of it either, as soldiers who had been pushed around at night could attest.

As we finished lunch and began setting up our equipment, we agreed to take the warning seriously. We had brought along our newest toy—a thermal-imaging camera that would show us variations in temperature in more dramatic terms than any electronic temperature gauge.

Grant and I headed for the room where the first sergeant had hung himself. At first, our thermal camera didn't pick up anything unusual. Then what looked like a mist passed in front of the lens. What surprised us wasn't just the presence of the mist—it was the fact that it registered as warmer than the surrounding air. Normally, mists are colder than the air.

Meanwhile, Steve, Brian, and Mike Dion had moved onto a catwalk that overlooked the building's big, hangar-like drill floor. It had been described to us as a place where a disproportionate number of cold spots had been detected. The guys were able to corroborate that by detecting some of them with their instruments.

They were trying to see if the cold spots were attributable to drafts when they realized their camera battery was draining at a ridiculous rate—as if something was sucking the energy out of it. They knew that supernatural entities need energy to manifest themselves and that they'll take it from any source they can find. Was their battery being used for that purpose?

Before they could draw any conclusions, something completely unexpected happened: Frank DeAngelis's feet went out from under him and he fell right on his back. Steve, who's a police officer, didn't know what had happened, but he was at Frank's side in a heartbeat.

"You okay, man?" he asked.

Frank didn't look like he could move. In a thin, terrified voice, he answered Steve's question. "No."

As he lay there, tears running down the sides of his face, Frank described what had happened to him. It had begun with a feeling of extreme cold. Then he'd felt something come up through the core of his body and yank his head back.

Right now, his chest felt like it had a weight on it, and his back hurt, and he was caught in the grip of a cold sweat. Steve, Brian, and Mike took their shirts off to keep him warm, knowing he might be going into shock—or worse.

A moment later, Rebello responded and took Frank's blood pressure. His breathing was quick and his heart rate was well into the hundreds, but it was gradually coming down. To everyone's relief, Frank wasn't in any serious danger.

When Grant and I got there, he was lying on his back, looking pale and sweaty and scared half to death. When we trained our thermal camera on his face, it showed inflammation under his chin, as if he had been struck by someone.

Finally, Frank felt well enough to get up. Grant and I took him to a room where we could debrief him in private.

Naturally, the investigators in us wanted to know exactly what had happened. But that wasn't our only reason for speaking with him.

Frank had been through a harrowing experience. He needed to talk about it, to get his feelings out in the open. To obtain some perspective.

After he had had some time to gather himself, he said it was an entity he had felt inside him. In his brief contact with it, he could feel what it was feeling, and it was full of negative emotions. He felt as if all his worst fears had been realized, as if doomsday were descending on him and there was nothing he could do about it.

At that point, it was six hours into the investigation. We called it a night. As we left, we told Rebello that we would be in touch as soon as we had a chance to go over the data.

When we did, it was nothing short of startling. Frank had said that he'd felt his head being jerked back. But in fact, he'd been hit by his audio equipment bag. Without warning or explanation, it had jumped up and slugged him under the chin.

We checked to make sure Frank hadn't inadvertently pulled the bag up with his hands. But we could see his hands and they were otherwise occupied. Besides, it was a heavy bag, and it wouldn't have been easy for him to yank it up that way.

When we returned to the armory, we met with Sergeant Rebello and his superior, Capt. Winfield Danielson. We told them what we had discovered. For one thing, we had detected the cold spots they mentioned. For another, we found that warm mist in the room where the first sergeant hanged himself.

However, the biggest piece of evidence was what had happened to Frank, all of which had been captured on videotape. In fact, it was the most violent documentation of the supernatural that either Grant or I had ever seen. Clearly, the Armory was host to legitimate paranormal activity.

But that wasn't the end of it. I still wanted to talk with Frank back at headquarters. Though from a medical standpoint he wasn't suffering any lasting effects, it would be naive to think he hadn't been damaged in some way.

"You may be changed by this," I told him. "I just want you to know that we're here for you."

Frank thanked me but decided not to go with us on any more investigations. He had had enough.

GRANT'S TAKE

What's scary is that what happened to Frank DeAngelis will eventually happen to all of us who pry into the paranormal. It's only a matter of time. We just have to hope that when it happens, we'll have the support we need from our families and colleagues to get through it.

LINGERING
OCTOBER 2004

Though we use a lot of different instruments when we check a site for paranormal activity, we also depend on our instincts. After all, we've been at this for a while, and we can usually tell when something's going on even without our collection of recorders and cameras and computer systems.

Then there are times when we're completely fooled. For instance, the night we visited the house of Adam Zubrowski in northern Connecticut.

Zubrowski, a friend of one of our cameramen on the show, was a pleasant enough guy with what sounded like a haunting problem. Every so often, he would hear a woman's voice in his house, even when there weren't any women present. This was especially true in the room where he kept his pool table, which had been his grandparents' bedroom before their deaths in 2000 and 2001. Zubrowski's grandparents, you see, had been the house's original residents. After they passed on, Adam became the sole owner of the place and all its contents.

But his grandparents hadn't just lived there. They had built the place, and gone on to build some of the furniture as well. What's more, their ashes were sitting in a container in the living room, so there was clearly a strong and intimate connection between Zubrowski's grandparents and his house.

Recently, he had woken up in the morning to find a bunch of bric-a-brac lying around his feet, nestled in the folds of his bedcovers. What freaked him out was that the stuff had been standing on his headboard when he went to sleep the night before. How had it gotten there? He hadn't the slightest idea.

His friends didn't either, but they knew enough about the place to stay away from it. One of them told us about the time he had stayed over in the back bedroom, where Adam's great-grandfather had died some years earlier. When the friend got a weird vibe in the middle of the night and heard a woman's voice whispering to him, he bolted from the house and refused to sleep over ever again.

There were other incidents. One time, a heavy oak fire door swung closed and locked itself on its own. Another time, Zubrowski went down into his basement and got the distinct feeling he wasn't alone. That was the last time he visited his basement on his own after dark.

"I used to be a skeptic," he told us. "But not anymore. I just want to know what's going on."

We tackled the Zubrowski residence with a team that included Brian Harnois, Steve Gonsalves, Heather Drolet, and Jen Rossi, in addition to Grant and myself. Jen, our archivist, was expanding her role in T.A.P.S. by training to be a field researcher.

Heather, who had brought her divining rods, was teamed with Brian and an EMF detector. The idea was to go over the reportedly active parts of the house with both modalities, to see if the rods and the detector came up with the same results.

They did and they didn't.

In the basement, for instance, Heather's brass rods crossed a bit, indicating some ambient energy. Brian's detector, on the other hand, showed nothing unusual. In the back bedroom, where Zubrowski's great-grandfather had passed on, neither Heather nor Brian came up with anything. It was only in the room with the pool table that Heather's rods registered a serious energy source, going so far as to form a perfect X when she placed them over the center of the table. But in the same room, Brian came up empty.

So, according to the divining rods, at least, there was activity. However, none of us felt anything out of the ordinary—not even Heather. When that's the case, it usually means we're barking up the wrong tree, and all we've done is encounter another homeowner with an overactive imagination.

We thanked Zubrowski, who had been a congenial host, and went back to Rhode Island. "Not a total loss," I told Grant on the way north. "At least Jen got some valuable investigative experience."

Then Brian and Steve sat down to go over the data, as they usually do. They were fully prepared to file an uneventful report. But when they examined our EVP recordings, they found something difficult to ignore.

Calling in Grant and me, they played the EVP for us. Though Zubrowski had described a woman's voice, this one seemed to belong to a man. Though the voice was labored, wheezing, the words were eerily clear: "I miss Adam." It sent a chill up my spine when I heard them.

We captured the voice again in another part of the tape. However, we couldn't make out the words this time. That was disappointing. When you get an EVP, you want to know what the heck it's saying.

Anyway, we brought the evidence back to Zubrowski's house and went over it with him. His dad was present, though he preferred to stand in the doorway that led to the kitchen, out of camera range.

When we played the "I miss Adam" EVP, Zubrowski's eyes opened wide. Obviously, he was moved by the idea that his grandfather was calling to him from the other side, expressing his longing for his beloved grandson. But it made sense, Zubrowski told us. He'd been very close with his grandparents, his grandfather in particular.

Then we played the other EVP, the one that sounded like gibberish to us. Before Zubrowski could comment, his father blurted out, "Oh, my God. It's Polish. He's speaking in *Polish*."

He went on to tell us that his father—Adam Zubrowski's grandfather—had died of a respiratory disease that had made it hard for him to breathe, which was why it sounded like the speaker of the EVP was struggling for air. The elder Zubrowski was caught up in a wave of emotion, grateful for the chance to hear his dad's voice again.

GRANT'S TAKE

What a moment that was—to hear Adam's father say that the EVP was a message in Polish. It's worth all the sweat and tears we put into our work when all the pieces fit the way they did that night. And we got to see not one but two generations of Zubrowskis make contact with the deceased.

HEADQUARTERS
FEBRUARY 2005

Early in 2005 we moved into our new headquarters. From the street it looks pretty much like any storefront, with vertical blinds covering the windows on either side of the front door—keeping the inquisitive from seeing what's inside. It could easily be the office of an accountant or a real estate broker or a bail bondsman.

Except for the fact that T.A.P.S. is stenciled on the glass.

Because we usually park in the lot behind the place, we don't use the front door much. Instead, we enter from the alley that runs between our office and the Chinese restaurant next door, where a previous tenant did himself in by guzzling battery acid.

In our business, we hear of a lot of grisly deaths, but battery acid . . .? You've really got to have some demons to even consider that as an option.

Not that our headquarters don't have their own check-ered past. In the office behind our conference room, which Grant and I share, a guy once blew his head off. It's a mira-cle we don't have a haunting of our own.

The front end of the office, which sits behind the door we seldom open, is mostly filled with desks and filing cabi-nets. However, there's no mistaking that this is T.A.P.S. ter-ritory. You can tell by the blown-up photos of a graveyard, a lighthouse, a prison—all places we've visited on one occa-sion or another.

We've also got a few humorous posters on the walls. One is a checklist of what to bring on an investigation: a flash-light, an EMF detector, spare batteries, a camera, and an ex-tra pair of shorts. Other posters say, "We scare them back," "I love the smell of ectoplasm in the morning," and "When Uncle Fred just won't go home . . ."

My favorite part of the office is the wall where we keep our dartboard. It's got three red-fletched darts in it, all near the bull's-eye, where I planted them. Alongside them is a shuriken, perhaps better known as a throw-ing star. I used to be into martial arts, and I'm pretty good at flinging that sucker. Not perfect, as the chewed-up patches of wall around the dartboard will attest, but good.

And of course, what would any office be without an ample supply of hand disinfectant? Hey, we've all got our personality quirks. Mine is I can't stand germs. I'm so bad I won't even touch the buttons in an elevator. And shaking hands? Don't get me started.

I know what you're thinking. How can a plumber, a guy who works with waste pipes, be so queasy about germs? Believe me, you're not the first person to ask. I just wish I had an answer.

Anyway, it's not the most luxurious place on the planet. I wouldn't have a cocktail reception there. But it sure beats working out of my basement, which is what we used to do.

GRANT'S TAKE

We only moved into our office a couple of years ago, but it already seems like we're outgrowing it. Every week, we've got a new set of recordings from a new bunch of cases, and only so many file cabinets to hold them. Pretty soon we'll have to build a warehouse.

THE MYRTLES
FEBRUARY 2005

One of the first conversations I had with my partner, Grant, in the conference room of our new
T.A.P.S. headquarters was really a reprise of an
old conversation: what to do with Brian Harnois. But then,
Brian's antics had been a recurring theme in our lives for
some time.

The latest problem was that Brian had missed a meeting
because he said he had to work. It was a lie, of course. He
often resorted to them when he was backed into a corner.
And I *knew* it was a lie because his boss was a friend of mine.
In fact, I had gotten Brian the job.

I tell you, Brian left us scratching our heads sometimes.
I considered him a good person and a close friend, or I
wouldn't have given him so much leeway in the past. But I
was kicking myself in the butt for that decision now.

135

Time and again, he misplaced or completely lost valuable equipment. Three times before, we had said good-bye to him only to grudgingly let him back into the group again. We couldn't do that anymore. As far as I was concerned, his days with us were numbered.

Fortunately for Brian, Grant had a soft spot for him. By the time we called him into the conference room later that day, I had been talked into taking a more flexible position—one I had a feeling I would come to regret. But Grant sounds so reasonable sometimes, it's hard to disagree with him.

GRANT'S TAKE

All I told Jason was that we ought to give Brian a chance to redeem himself. We needed to clearly set out his duties and the penalties for not fulfilling them. Then, if he screwed up, it was all on him.

Brian entered the room like a child who had been caught with his hand in the cookie jar. "You're hurting the whole group," I told him. "We were going to let you go, but we've reconsidered."

Up to that point, Brian's promises to do better had been sealed with a handshake. That wasn't going to fly anymore. We presented him with a code of conduct that laid out everything he had to do or steer clear of in order to remain in the organization. The penalties for diverging from the code ran the gamut from Brian's being disciplined to his being dismissed.

It was the only way we could keep him on this time—we emphasized that. Then we asked him to read and sign the code of conduct. "Screw up and you're gone," I advised him, just for good measure.

You could see that Brian was shaken up. T.A.P.S. was his life, he said. He even had a T.A.P.S. tattoo on his arm. He had spent six years with the organization. He didn't want to see all that go up in smoke.

Meanwhile, we had gotten some terrific news from Donna. The owners of The Myrtles, a former plantation turned bed-and-breakfast hotel in the Louisiana bayou, had asked us to come down and test the claim that the place was haunted.

Grant and I could barely contain ourselves. The Myrtles was known as one of the most haunted places in America. It was every paranormal investigator's dream to check the place out.

We asked Brian to come with us because he would have killed us if we hadn't. But given the magnitude of the case, we hedged our bet. Instead of putting Brian in charge of the equipment, we asked Steve to assume that role.

Steve was only too glad to take on the added responsibility, but he didn't want to step on anyone's toes. "What about Brian?" he asked. "Don't worry about him," I said, knowing Brian would agree to pretty much anything at that point.

It was a three-day trip down to New Orleans by car. Steve and Brian would take our new mobile command center, a van outfitted with all the monitors and hard drives we would need in an investigation, which allowed us to eliminate a good half hour of setup time.

Jen Rossi would drive one of our other vehicles. What

better place for her to get more field experience than The Myrtles?

We would also send Paula Donovan and Kristyn Gartland down there. Kristyn was a field researcher for T.A.P.S. We had originally met her seven or eight years earlier when her house was plagued by a poltergeist. Paula was a research scientist, who was by nature a bit more skeptical. We figured Paula's analytical mind would be an asset in this investigation. Kristyn, with her understanding of both people and equipment, had proven herself a valuable member of the team as well.

Soon after Grant and I arrived at the airport, we began the three-and-a-half-hour trek to The Myrtles, which was in St. Francisville, Louisiana, about halfway between New Orleans and Natchez, Mississippi. It was beautiful in the bayous. The time flew by so quickly that we were at the gates to the old plantation before we knew it.

It was about as elegant a place as I had ever seen, with its classical statuary, its towering oak trees, and its 120-foot-long veranda. As we drove up, we were met by Teeta Moss, the owner. She welcomed us to the main house, which had been built in 1794 and was on the National Historical Register.

The Myrtles had become known as a haunted property, Moss said, but she wanted concrete evidence, and T.A.P.S. had gained a reputation for credibility in the field. We promised to check the place out as thoroughly as we could. To be honest, I was just hoping we didn't break any stained-glass windows.

Though The Myrtles had eleven guest rooms, none of them had a television or a radio. The plantation hadn't changed in more than two hundred years. It was stuck squarely in the past.

Hester Eby, who had spoken to Donna on the phone, was the manager of the property. She took us to a flagstone path between two buildings, where she said an all-but-transparent figure had been seen. People have identified the figure as Cloe, a slave back in the days when The Myrtles was a working plantation.

According to legend, Cloe was the plantation owner's mistress. When he ended their affair for reasons of his own, she began spying on his family. Eventually he caught her and punished her by cutting off her ear. Then he sent her into the fields to work like all the other slaves.

In time, Cloe managed to work her way back into her master's good graces, so when a family birthday came up, she was the one given the responsibility of baking the birthday cake. But along with all the other ingredients, she put in a small amount of poison. In one version of the story, she did this to get her revenge. In another, she wanted to make the master's children sick so she would have to return to his house to take care of them.

In any event, the master's wife and two children ate the entire cake and instantly fell ill. Ironically, it was Cloe who was asked to care for them and nurse them back to health. However, the poison proved too much for them. All three of them died.

Cloe was put to death for her crime, but not at the hands of the plantation owner. As the story goes, she was hanged by her fellow slaves, who feared their master's wrath. It was said she still hangs around the plantation owner's house, hoping to be readmitted into his good graces.

But she wasn't alone. The ghosts of the plantation owner's wife and two children were believed to haunt the place as well. According to witnesses, they showed up not only on the property but also in the house.

Hester took us inside to tell us about a couple of other ghostly legends. For instance, a mirror with metallic-looking smudges. Photographs of it supposedly showed the shapes of two small children in the top left corner. Were they the ghosts of the children Cloe had killed? No one knew.

Next we walked through the lady's parlor. One time, when Hester was leading a tour there, she felt the tug of a child on her arm. But when she turned to see who it might be, there was no one there.

Outside, there was a pond covered with a solid-looking layer of tiny green leaves. It was an innocent enough scene. But photos of it had revealed what looked like a Confederate soldier standing at the water's edge.

And then there was the story of William Wincher, a West Virginian infantryman during the Civil War, who, when a guest at The Myrtles, was shot in the chest by an unidentified assailant. Crawling into the main house through the side door, he tried desperately to find his wife, Sarah. Wincher made it as far as the staircase's seventeenth step, but no farther. Fortunately, Sarah heard his calls and embraced him before he expired.

Footsteps had been heard on the stairs from time to time. Did they belong to the ghost of William Wincher? We hoped to shed some light on the question.

Other activity at the plantation included the spirit of a French woman who wandered from room to room, an entity who played the same chord over and over again on the grand piano, a portrait that changed expressions, and an apparition of a girl who only appeared before storms.

One thing we didn't show in our TV coverage of The Myrtles was a photograph someone had taken—one of many in the owner's files—that showed evidence of the supernatural. In the photo, we could see what looked like the ghost of a female slave standing between two of the plantation's buildings.

The Myrtles people wanted the image of the female cleaned up so it could be determined what she looked like. They ended up sending it to a "paranormal guy." His job was simply to make the ghostly image more distinct.

But he did more than that. He tampered with it.

When he was done, you could see not only the image of the woman but something else as well—the shadows of two children sitting on a branch, just to the right of the apparition. Except there were no shadows of any kind in the original photo. There was just a clapboard surface.

More than likely, the guy was trying to help The Myrtles maintain its reputation as a haunted house. Instead, he cast doubt on what had been a pretty compelling piece of evidence.

Obviously, there were a lot of stories to prove or disprove at The Myrtles. Grant, who can be like a kid sometimes, was stressed because he didn't want to miss any of them. But we had to be realistic. We decided to focus on just the spots with the most reported activity.

Hester left us with an ominous remark: "Many guests have left us before the night is over." We promised her we would be there until morning.

First off, G.W. and I looked at the mirror Hester had

shown us. It looked like it had been handled quite a bit, which would mean it had been exposed to the acids in people's fingertips. That might be what had created the mysterious shapes beneath its glass surface.

Then it was a matter of what people saw in the shapes. Matrixing is the tendency of the human mind to fill in details where there are gaps, making us see things that aren't there. We guessed it was this phenomenon that made the children seem to appear in photographs of the mirror.

While Jen sat down in our mobile command center to watch the monitors, Paula and Kristyn explored the grounds and the slave shack. At the same time, Steve and Brian finished setting up the cameras. Then they went to the dining room of the main house to record some audio impressions.

After they left, Grant and I went into the house to scan the place with our thermal camera. In particular, we wanted to check out the area around the stairwell, where people had heard footsteps. It turned out to be a good idea.

As we stood at the top of the stairs, something moved past our camera—something warmer than its surroundings, judging by its yellow thermal color. We couldn't make out any details, but it seemed to have moved up in front of the lens and then to our right. With luck, we would get a better idea of what it was when we analyzed the footage back in our hotel room.

In the meantime, Paula and Kristyn were investigating the area around the side door where Wincher had been shot. Their EMF readings started out low but quickly climbed when they got to a particular spot. Kristyn, especially, was excited about their results—until she realized there was an electrical box in the vicinity. "Damn it," she muttered good-naturedly, "I hate when that happens. Stupid electrical box."

By eleven o'clock, Steve and Brian were out walking the grounds of the plantation, approaching a gazebo where a couple of phenomena had been reported: the sight of a Civil War–era soldier strolling the grounds as if he were still alive, and the voices of kids playing. They both sounded like a residual haunting—the kind that repeats over and over again. In any case, Steve was playing his flashlight up ahead, hoping to catch a glimpse of something.

At the same time, I was checking out the slave shack with Grant. We noticed that there wasn't any camera in it, even though we had given Brian specific instructions to set one up in there. Grant gave Brian a call, letting him know about his oversight.

To Brian's credit, he promised he would address it right away—and did. But that left Steve to go on exploring the grounds by himself.

Normally, no one goes off on his or her own during an investigation. The T.A.P.S. rule is that we proceed in pairs or threes, but never by ourselves. In fact, when this case aired as a television episode, we got all kinds of e-mails about the inadvisability of Steve's little solo adventure.

Remember, though—if you can see him on television, he's not alone. There's a *cameraman* with him. So in reality, Steve wasn't breaking any rules. He had all the company he needed.

But after a while, he got a little more—in the form of a flitting shadow. Without hesitation, he pursued it through the darkness, trying to get a video recording of it. Unfortunately, it ducked behind a tree and got away.

When Brian rejoined him, Steve told him what he had seen. As they continued their pursuit, Brian saw something as well. But as before, it proved elusive.

All evening, we heard a dog barking in the distance, getting on our nerves. After Steve and Brian lost the shadow, Steve heard the dog bark again. He yelled, "Shut up your damn dog!" Normally, he's a pretty quiet guy, so it was a surprise to hear him shout like that. But the bigger surprise was that the dog stopped barking. In fact, we didn't hear a peep from it the rest of the night.

At this point, Grant and I were exploring the grounds as well, but with the benefit of our thermal camera. We were down in the area of the pond when, without warning, something flashed in front of our lens. When we replayed it in the camera, it looked vaguely human—except you could see through it.

We remained in that spot for a while and tried to capture it again, but to no avail. It was pushing two in the morning when we made our last stop—the slave shack. By then, Grant and I were happy to just sit and chill.

The subject of Brian came up again. I'd had to speak to him twice about setting up a camera there in the shack. It seemed like a small thing, but every camera was important. You never knew which one was going to record something remarkable.

At one point, I felt the air pressure increase in my ears. Grant felt the same thing. But we didn't think much of it.

By 2:20, we had exhausted the subject of Brian and were on to a more philosophical one. "Ever wonder," I asked my partner, "if we're doing the right thing?" In other words, was our approach to ghost hunting the valid one? "How much time and energy do we expend before we burn bridges we can never repair?"

I was fatigued and I wasn't expressing myself very well, but G.W. knew exactly what I meant. We had made sacrifices in our personal and working lives to pursue something we believed in. When the dust cleared, would we regret what we had given up? Would we still have our families, our jobs, our self-respect?

The whole point was to have people accept paranormal investigation as a legitimate scientific endeavor. But there was no guarantee that would ever happen, let alone in our lifetimes.

We were so tired and so engrossed in our conversation that we were completely oblivious to what was happening in the slave shack. Fortunately, our camera was rolling, recording what was going on behind our backs.

At 3:00, we decided to hit the sack. We had covered all the spots we had targeted for investigation and gotten some interesting results. But Steve and Brian would keep the cameras running until morning, sleeping in shifts so that there was always someone to watch the equipment.

In the morning, we packed up. Hester thanked us and said she was eager to hear what we had found. Reluctantly, we left The Myrtles behind and drove back through the gates of the property and into the bayou country.

Meanwhile, Brian had done a credible job. He'd had to be reminded a couple of times about one thing or another, but he had generally acquitted himself well. It was good to see.

At the motel outside New Orleans, Steve, Jen, and Brian began going over the footage we had taken: thirty hours of video and an additional ten hours of audio. It was tedious at first, as it always is when you can't find anything out of the ordinary. Then something popped at them.

At about 3:20, after everyone but Steve and Brian went to sleep, we got something from the camera we had left shooting down the stairs in the main house: a shadow on the other side of a translucent glass door that looked a lot like a human figure. I wondered out loud if it could have been a member of our team casting the shadow, but we were all accounted for at the time. So that was something worth discussing.

But it wasn't the coup de grace. That came when they were checking out the footage from the slave shack. There was a table between Grant and me that had a nice lace cover and a lamp sitting on top of it. As we watched the video, we saw the lamp slowly but surely slide to the right, and it didn't stop until it had moved a good fourteen inches.

When Grant and I saw it, we were flabbergasted. We'd been right there when the lamp had moved, yet we hadn't noticed a thing. It was a pretty impressive piece of evidence.

However, we didn't want to jump to any unwarranted conclusions. After all, Grant might have snagged the lamp cord with his foot and dragged it without knowing it. We decided we had to go back to the plantation and take a closer look at the room.

But when we examined the lamp, the table, and the slave shack in broad daylight, we couldn't find another explanation. We had to attribute the phenomenon to a supernatural force.

In other words, the place was haunted. Grant and I

agreed on that. Our report put a smile on Hester's face. She had believed all along that there were ghosts inhabiting the plantation, and now she had her proof.

As we left The Myrtles, Grant and I remarked on the funny way events had unfolded in the slave shack. We had been having doubts about ghost hunting and the immense toll it took on our lives. But finding exciting evidence like the moving lamp had given us a fresh start, a second wind.

Once again, we were ready for anything.

GRANT'S TAKE

If we were looking for a sign that we were doing something worthwhile, we couldn't have asked for a better one than that lamp. And it happened right behind our backs. It just goes to show—no matter how experienced you are, you can miss something if you're not paying attention.

MULTIPLE HAUNTINGS
FEBRUARY 2005

There are three kinds of hauntings. The first kind is residual—when a supernatural entity repeats the same act over and over again. The second kind is intelligent—when an entity is aware of its actions and can interact with the living. The third kind is poltergeist activity—when an entity moves objects in the physical world.

In Cranston, Rhode Island, we encountered claims of all three.

The DiRaimo family was the one making the claims. Ken DiRaimo, his wife, and his two daughters had been experiencing what seemed like supernatural phenomena for two decades, since shortly after the girls were born. They had all heard the voice of a woman in the house, and Hayley, one of the DiRaimos' daughters, even believed she had seen her.

She described the woman as brown-skinned with no feet.

There was no one ahead of us as we ascended the stairs . . . or was there?

Jason thought he was alone. This picture would seem to indicate otherwise.

There on the stairs—a shadow! But whose is it and what is it doing there?

Sometimes we just can't resist clowning around—like when we visited the house of alleged ax murderer Lizzie Borden.

Eastern State Penitentiary is still haunted by the souls of those who perished there.

St. Augustine Lighthouse looked innocent enough—but it was plenty creepy inside.

The Crescent Hotel still echoes with the suffering of Norman Baker's victims.

Here's the T.A.P.S. van in front of the battleship *North Carolina*. A lot of things happened onboard ship that we couldn't explain.

T.A.P.S. uses scientific methods to determine whether or not someone's home might be haunted. Photographs like this one give us a lot to consider.

The real work starts after we get back to headquarters and review our data. Here's Jason with Steve Gonsalves, our technology manager.

These shadows were all too visible to our camera, but not to the naked eye.

There's someone at the far end of the closet . . . but all our people are otherwise accounted for.

A bizarre trick of the light…or evidence of a supernatural entity? You be the judge.

Ghosts aren't particular. Warehouses and industrial sites can be haunted too.

We often detect orbs, but we don't accept them as evidence of a haunting.

The EMF detector records jumps in electromagnetic activity, and helps us rule out false positives generated by surrounding equipment.

She had walked across the foot of Hayley's bed and into her vanity mirror, at which point the woman had vanished. However, Hayley's bed and the mirror had begun to shake.

More rarely, she had heard a male voice. Hayley claimed to have seen the source of that as well—a man with a white face and black clothing. However, he had made his appearance in the kitchen, not a bedroom.

On another occasion in the kitchen, Hayley had seen the drawers and cabinet doors open and close several times. She had also seen a bust of William Shakespeare, which sat in the living room, turn as much as ninety degrees. And a friend of hers had been pushed down the stairs from behind.

People had told Hayley she was nuts. She wanted T.A.P.S. to capture something—anything—that would prove she hadn't taken leave of her senses.

In addition to Steve, Brian, and Paula, we had two other T.A.P.S. members with us that night. One was Dustin Pari. The second was Jill Raczelowski, our archivist. Jill loved to take part in investigations, though she depended more on her feelings than on scientific observation and analysis.

We took some time to set up our cameras, including one trained on the bust of Shakespeare. Then we went through the house with EMF detectors and established base ratings for those rooms where activity had been reported. Because the house was a tight fit, we sent a couple of people out to the van—also known as our mobile command center—with our digital video recorder.

We had barely gotten underway when I felt a burning sensation in the area of my shoulder blade. It was as if someone had been holding a match to it. I had my hands full just keeping my composure and not alarming the family, who had been alarmed enough.

First chance I got, I excused myself and went upstairs to take off my shirt. Underneath, the skin looked as if it had been sunburned or rubbed raw. It wasn't a small area, either. It was easily the size of my hand.

I had never felt anything like it before, and I never wanted to feel it again. But it told me one thing: there was definitely some activity in this house. Before we left, we needed to prove it.

However, we didn't seem to be having much luck. No voices, no moving objects, nothing that would support the family's claims. We made the observation that Hayley seemed to be the focus of all the activity in the house. Someone—Paula, I think—came up with the idea of taking Hayley up to her room with us.

So Hayley came up and sat on her bed with Paula, and asked the spirits in the room for a sign of their presence. A moment later, Hayley said her right arm felt cold, as if it had been exposed to a freezing wind. Brian, who was standing nearby, wanted to see if it was just a subjective sensation or if Hayley's arm had really gotten colder. With his digital thermometer, he took a reading of the affected area.

"Sixty-nine degrees," he announced.

Colder than it should have been, but not ridiculously so. Then Hayley said she felt chills in her spine and in one of her legs. Again, Brian took a reading. This time, it was forty degrees.

Finally, it was time to wrap. We took our thirty-plus hours of recordings and went back to Warwick. On the way, Grant and I recapped the action.

We hadn't gathered anything in the way of hard evidence. I had the burn or whatever it was. Hayley's leg had gotten cold. Both occurrences were inexplicable. However, neither of them was proof of a supernatural presence.

Brian and Steve started the analysis the next day. By evening, they were ready to show us what they had found—which was basically nothing. The bust of Shakespeare hadn't moved. The cabinet doors in the kitchen hadn't swung open. We hadn't sighted any apparitions or picked up any EVPs.

Sometimes you don't find anything, as much as you would like to. That's the way it goes in this business. But Brian and Steve had gone through more than thirty hours of footage in ten hours.

The way they had things set up, they could look at four video sources at once. But how closely could they have examined those sources? Not very. And sometimes two seconds of footage makes a whole investigation worthwhile.

When we confronted Brian and Steve, they admitted that they had rushed through the analysis. Brian in particular had fast-forwarded through much of his footage. Grant and I weren't satisfied. We asked them to start from scratch and do the job right this time.

Steve said he would do as we asked. Brian grumbled a little but eventually agreed as well. Then Grant and I rethought the situation.

If Brian had shirked his responsibility the first time, why should we have any confidence he would do it right the second time? It wasn't fair to the DiRaimos to give them anything less than our best. In the end, Grant and I decided to go over the footage ourselves. It was good that we did.

Partway through the analysis, Grant took off his earphones and looked at me. "I think I've got something," he said.

I listened to the audio. There was a voice, all right—a male voice. Not much more than a whisper, but it was there. "Have them go," it said. I played it again, just to make sure. Again I heard, "Have them go."

When we played the tape for the DiRaimos, they agreed: it was a man's voice saying, "Have them go." Was the voice talking about our T.A.P.S. team? It seemed like a reasonable assumption.

There was still a question as to what was causing the activity in the house. Was it Hayley? We couldn't say. But it was clear that she was pleased with our results.

She had proof now. No one could call her crazy.

GRANT'S TAKE

In the early days of T.A.P.S., Jason and I would often do the analyses ourselves. However, we had long since turned that part of the investigation over to other people, mainly Steve and Brian—guys who had demonstrated a knack for finding a needle of evidence in a haystack of data. It was only because they fell short this time that we reprised our old roles.

THE GREEN-EYED MONSTER
FEBRUARY 2005

Jealous women seemed to be the theme when we went down to New Orleans to help Bruce DeVille, who claimed he had a female spirit in his house that kept scaring off his lady friends. We were brought to the case by Pam Gates of Southern Louisiana Ghost Hunters, another member of the T.A.P.S. family, who believed DeVille's stories were credible but lacked evidence to prove their veracity.

In fact, she had felt a push from behind when she investigated the DeVille house weeks earlier. So it wasn't just her analysis of the situation that led her to call T.A.P.S. She was going by personal experience.

Because of the nature of the case, we brought two women with us from Rhode Island, Kristyn Gartland and Paula Donovan, both of whom had accompanied us to The Myrtles.

Even before we got out of the airport, we had trouble. Brian and Steve had driven down to Louisiana with our equipment to meet us at the airport and take us to DeVille's place. However, they had a flat tire on the way and showed up late.

Normally, I wouldn't have given them grief for it (well, not too much), but Brian was already on my bad side. His girlfriend, whom he had met because of his involvement with T.A.P.S., was on his cell phone with him constantly, bugging him about spending so much time with us and not enough with her. Every time I turned around, Brian was bent over his phone instead of doing his work.

Anyway, it didn't take long to get from the airport to DeVille's place. But just before we got there, we saw a neighbor point a shotgun at us. If we ventured onto his property, he told us, he would shoot us. We told him we were headed for the DeVille house and had no intention of trespassing on his land, but that didn't seem to calm him down. If anything, it got him riled up even more.

We were still thinking about the guy when we pulled up in front of DeVille's residence—a white frame house with green trim on land that had once been part of a sugarcane plantation. DeVille, a spare man with a dark mustache, said that as long as he had been bringing girlfriends to the house, they had never felt comfortable there. When we asked him for background on the place, he said a woman had died there some years before his family moved in.

DeVille's brother and sister lived in the house as well. His sister had periodically been plagued by shadows and voices in her bedroom. His brother's room sometimes smelled like what DeVille described as "death." And DeVille himself had felt someone crawl into bed with him in the middle of the night, though when he turned to see who it was there was no one there.

He also claimed to have encountered the ghost of a Cajun girl in his room. Pam backed him up, saying she believed she had seen the girl as well. Creeped out by the experience, DeVille had since moved to another room.

DeVille's brother, a big, innocent-looking guy, turned out to be a fan of our TV show and of me in particular. He had even shaved his head to resemble me more closely. As luck would have it, his name was Jason too.

More than anything, DeVille wanted the spirit out of his house. Clearly, it was putting a crimp in his social calendar. But beyond that, he just wanted to lead a normal life.

Our plan was to have Kristyn remain with DeVille in his room in the hope that the spirit would get jealous and do something we could get on tape. We would have a camera running in that room, another in the room where the woman had died, and two more in DeVille's sister's room. It seemed like a sound approach, but it hit a snag almost right away.

From the time Kristyn entered the house, she felt uncomfortable and weighted down. She wasn't a woman who was easily scared off, but in this case she said she didn't want to stay there with DeVille. So we went to Plan B—a friend of DeVille's named Ashley Smith, who was kind enough to come over and serve as our spirit-bait.

As she sat down with DeVille, Brian and Steve went off

to explore DeVille's old bedroom for evidence of the little Cajun girl, who called herself Genevieve. Before too long, the two of them started to feel tingly, a sign that there was something or someone in the room with them.

It was then that they saw a shadow move in the corner. One that looked human.

But they only glimpsed it for a second. After that, it was gone. Looking more closely, they found a board missing in the floor, but it wasn't clear if there was a connection between the girl and the missing board.

One thing was certain: the longer Brian and Steve stayed in the room, the colder they felt. They started feeling dizzy too. And it seemed to them that something was weighing them down. But they couldn't pick up anything with their EMF detector.

By midnight, we still hadn't found any manifestations in DeVille's room. We decided to swap Pam for Ashley and see what would happen. Meanwhile, Kristyn and Paula were checking out DeVille's sister's room. They felt uncomfortable as soon as they entered it, Kristyn more than Paula. Paula did detect some cold spots with her EMF detector, but they turned out to be the result of interference from a halogen lamp.

A bigger problem was the nonstop static Brian was getting from his girlfriend. It was getting to the point where I didn't want him around. I told Grant as much, and, as sympathetic as he can be at times, he didn't disagree.

In any case, it was time to pack up and see what we had gotten. We thanked DeVille for his hospitality and retreated to a nearby motel, where Brian and Steve began the laborious process of going over the data.

Sometimes they pore over tapes for hours and come up empty-handed. Fortunately, this wasn't one of those times. Calling Grant and me into their room, they showed us footage of a door in DeVille's house. For a while, it just stood there. Then it opened all by itself. And a moment later, it closed.

In fact, it did it twice, though it didn't open quite as far the second time. Grant and I looked at each other. We had the same thought: to go back to DeVille's and take a look at that door.

Our approach, remember, is to try to debunk what seems like evidence of the paranormal. But when we returned to the house and examined the door, we couldn't explain its opening and closing any other way. It was a heavy door on tight hinges, so it wasn't going to be moved by an errant breeze. It was a nice piece of documentation.

Unfortunately, it was the only piece we got. But Kristyn had experienced some feelings she wouldn't soon forget. And our going down there had cemented our bond with our sister group in Louisiana.

More importantly, our research enabled us to make a recommendation to Bruce DeVille. Conversations with his brother, Jason, had revealed that they were at odds when it came to the entity in their house. As much as Bruce wanted to be rid of it, Jason was fascinated by it and wanted it to stay.

It only takes one member of a household to make a spirit feel welcome. And as long as it felt welcome, it wasn't going anywhere.

Grant advised DeVille to come to an agreement with his brother about the entity. "Get together and make it a family effort," he said. "Put your foot down. Tell the ghost to move on. Take back your house."

GRANT'S TAKE

To this point, I had taken Brian's side whenever Jason got fed up with him. But his conversations with his girlfriend had become a thorn in our side. I couldn't defend him anymore.

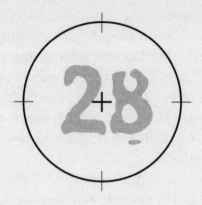

THE HAUNTED DINING ROOM
FEBRUARY 2005

Most people know Brennan's restaurant in New Orleans' French Quarter as one of the country's finest dining establishments. But it wasn't the food that brought us to Brennan's on the second and last stop of our Big Easy trip. It was the claim that the place was haunted.

We were invited there by the Brennan family, the owners of the 212-year-old restaurant. Unfortunately, I was sick with the worst head cold of my life on the night we were supposed to check out Brennan's. We ended up postponing the investigation until the following night, when I was feeling a little better.

David Sledd, the captain, met us at the Royal Street entrance and gave us a tour of the place, starting with dinner in the infamous Red Room. As we sampled Cajun-Creole dishes under a gas-burning chandelier, Sledd directed our attention to the portraits hanging on the walls.

One depicted a Mr. LeFleur, a local shipping magnate. Another showed his wife and a third one showed his son. As the story goes, LeFleur went out one morning and arranged for three funerals. Then he went home and methodically killed his wife and child before hanging himself from the Red Room's chandelier.

The portrait of LeFleur is said to change expression every time you look at it, going from a smile to an angry scowl to a troubled frown and back again. I might have been able to see it if my head hadn't been so stuffed.

Sledd pointed out a cold spot over the fireplace in the room, which all six of us got a chance to experience for ourselves. It was cold there all right, though the debunker in me wondered if there was a hole nearby that a draft could come through.

Apparently, the LeFleur story has been an unlucky one, and not just for the LeFleurs. One night, as Sledd was telling the tale to a bunch of kids in the Red Room, a young riverboat captain put on a sheet and burst into the room. The kids were scared out of their shoes, as expected. But that night the captain, who was only twenty-seven, died in his sleep.

After dinner, we were shown the Chantelclair Room. Once, when it was being painted, the painters looked out the window and saw the face of an old woman. They all ran out and set off a night alarm. But when the police responded, they didn't find anyone outside the room.

Sledd also told us about sightings of apparitions and occasions when people heard dishes banging though no one was banging them. Then he let us go to work. As always, we set up our equipment and began our investigation.

Paula and Kristyn checked out the Chantelclair Room while Steve and Brian took a look at the Red Room. However, neither team could get much done because there was a party on the same floor. Over the course of the next several hours, we tried our best to pick up evidence supporting the restaurant's claims, but we couldn't find a thing.

It was an unfortunate situation. Brennan's had shut down the restaurant for us the first night, but there were customers in it the second night. It really inhibited the possibility of a valid investigation.

It didn't help that Brian had spent half the time on the phone with his girlfriend. Clearly, we would have to have a talk with him. He was going to have to make a choice between his girlfriend and his position in T.A.P.S.

As for Brennan's, I would like to go back there some day, and not just for the food. I can't help wondering what we would find.

GRANT'S TAKE

I really regretted not being able to investigate Brennan's the way we would have liked. Unfortunately, Jason and I are human, and like everyone else we get sick once in a while. In fact, the way we run around pursuing case after case, it's a wonder we don't get sick more often.

THE IOO-YEAR-OLD PLAYHOUSE
FEBRUARY 2005

T heaters always make for fun investigations. Maybe it's because we're all frustrated actors and we love to be on stage. Or maybe it's because the ghosts there are so . . . well, theatrical. At any rate, we were looking forward to hunting ghosts at the century-old Bradley Playhouse in Putnam, Connecticut.

Partly because the place was so close to our headquarters in Warwick, and partly because we wanted to get a couple of people some experience, we brought along a bigger team than usual. In addition to Brian, Steve, Donna, Grant, and me, we had on hand Paula Donovan from our research and development department and Jill Raczelowski, our T.A.P.S. archivist.

The Bradley Playhouse had seen its share of trouble, mostly in the form of fires. The first two had taken place in 1914, just fourteen hours apart. The damage had come to $40,000, which was a huge sum at the time. In 1937, the theater suffered another enormous blaze, the result of a short circuit in an actress's dressing room. Had it not been for an experimental asbestos curtain, the whole building would have gone up in flames.

Pat Green, who ran the place, greeted us at the door when we arrived. She told us about the phenomena reported by actors, stage crew, and patrons over the years. The actors, for instance, claimed to have seen an entity running behind them when they were on stage.

They had also seen a woman standing in the balcony after the audience had left the theater. It had happened so often that they had given her a name: Victoria. Figures had also been seen flitting by in the mirrors that lined the wall opposite the stage.

Pat Green took us into one of the dressing rooms, which had a creepy, Victorian feeling to it. A lady in a white dress had been glimpsed there from time to time. People had also heard noises in the theater that they couldn't explain.

We thanked our tour guide and started setting up our equipment. It was a big theater, with nearly a thousand seats, but it didn't seem to offer too many logistical problems. Besides, we had a lot of hands to help out.

Most of the time, I'm the one who pulls the practical jokes during an investigation. This time, Donna tried to take my place. She had gotten hold of a remote-control fart machine—a device that made farting sounds whenever she hit a button—and had hidden it in our Yukon sport utility vehicle.

On the way to Putnam, Grant and I were sitting in the

Yukon and talking, filming a segment of the show, and in the background there were these farting noises. Donna was setting them off from her car, snickering to herself. But we had an idea of what was going on and we ignored the farts. We just kept filming.

We didn't say anything about it, either. But when we got to the playhouse, we found the fart machine and took out the batteries. So when Donna came to check on it, wondering why it hadn't worked, she would find a reason.

Later, while we were setting up in the theater, we put the batteries back in. Then we had one of our production guys hide the machine under the springs of Donna's car and steal her remote for us. When we saw her, we asked her to film a shot where she drives up to the theater in her car. "No problem," she said. But as she pulled up to the curb, we used our stolen remote to set off the machine. All she heard were these long, loud, wet farts.

She couldn't believe it. It was a total backfire. That will teach her to mess with the master.

In the meantime, our setup wasn't going as quickly as we expected. I went to see why—and found Brian talking on his cell phone. Naturally, he was talking with his girlfriend.

Steve was unhappy because he felt that Brian was slacking off. Not one to mince words, Steve expressed his resentment. I, in turn, confronted Brian, asking him what was more important than his obligations to T.A.P.S.

Brian felt he was still doing his job, and balked at any innuendo to the contrary. But there was no denying that he was taking a long time to finish the setup. And the longer it took, the less time we would have to investigate.

In the meantime, Paula was running past the mirrors on

the wall, trying to see if she could debunk the claim that images were seen flitting by in the reflective surfaces. Unfortunately, she couldn't find an angle from which her reflection could be seen without her being seen also. But it was a good try.

Soon after, we were ready to go dark. Killing the lights, we proceeded with the rest of the investigation. Brian and Steve conducted an EVP sweep of the playhouse basement, which didn't turn up any unusual sounds. However, they did find a trapdoor. It was an exciting discovery until they opened it and found nothing but a concrete surface underneath it.

Donna and Jill started their efforts in the playhouse office. When they couldn't find anything there, they moved on to the balcony, where, with audio equipment in hand, they looked for Victoria. Donna, who is sensitive to such things, felt a sadness up there, but no scientific evidence.

At the same time, Grant and I were discussing the actors' claims. We were skeptical about something running behind the actors when they were on stage. After all, there were people in the audience. If the actors could see these things, why didn't anyone in the audience remark on them?

We also tested the acoustics of the place to see how small a noise could be heard from a distance. We discovered big honking air vents offstage that would kick on at strange times and make weird sounds. Certainly, they would provide an explanation of the noises people had heard.

Up in the balcony, Steve, Brian, and Paula were using an EMF detector to see if they could find any energy fluctuations. Five hours into the investigation, they ran into a 4.0

spike, which is a serious variation. But try as they might, they couldn't find a repeat of it.

Soon after that, we called it a night.

Back at headquarters, Steve and Brian ran through the footage and found only one piece of evidence. As they and Paula were talking in front of one of our cameras, an orb seemed to appear and linger for a while. Was it in fact an orb or something else? That was the question they asked themselves as they reexamined the tape. Eventually, they decided it was just a dust mote.

That left Grant and me with a problem. Pat Green had been really nice to us, and we hated to tell her we hadn't turned up any proof the place was haunted. There are ghost-hunting groups who make money off their investigations and tell their clients whatever they want to hear. T.A.P.S. isn't one of them.

So we went back to the theater and sat down with Pat Green. Unfortunately, we said, we hadn't come up with any evidence supporting the theater's claims. To our surprise, she was fine with that. In fact, she was relieved. Now she could relax when she found herself alone at night in the theater.

From our point of view, the investigation had been profitable, even if we hadn't run into any ghosts. After all, we had accomplished some good debunking, and, as Grant will tell you, that's as satisfying to us as anything else is.

We were all ready to head for home when we got a call from Brian. He wanted to talk with us for a minute. That was good, I told Grant, because I wanted to talk with him too. This business with his girlfriend and his cell phone had gone far enough.

When we met Brian in a park near our headquarters, I had a whole list of things to tell him. Uncharacteristically, he insisted on speaking first. That's when he dropped his bomb on us: he wanted to take a leave of absence from T.A.P.S.

Why? He claimed he felt intimidated by me. I told Brian that his problems were of his own making. He had allowed his relationship with his girlfriend to warp everything else in his life.

On one case alone, he had spent three hours talking on his cell. Worse, when anyone confronted him about his problem, he took refuge in a lie. One time when Steve told him he needed to get off the phone, he said he was speaking to me—but he wasn't. He was speaking to his girlfriend.

If he wanted a leave of absence, that was fine with me. Grant too. I felt bad that the situation had come to this, but it seemed like the best decision for everyone concerned. So Brian left.

Grant and I sat there for a while, talking about what Brian's departure would mean to T.A.P.S. In a way, we were relieved. But we also recognized that we had lost a work-horse and, more than that, a friend.

GRANT'S TAKE

It was sad saying good-bye to Brian. He had worked with us almost from the beginning, helping to build T.A.P.S. into a highly regarded ghost-hunting operation. But it was time to make a change.

MORDECAI HOUSE
MARCH 2005

Most of the time T.A.P.S. is so busy we have to train people on the run. Other times, we have some time on our hands. It doesn't happen often, believe me. But when it does, we like to set up a pure training run.

No pressure, plenty of leeway to make mistakes. That was what we had in mind as we left rainy Rhode Island in a three-vehicle caravan and headed down to North Carolina, where we were slated to investigate Mordecai House, the birthplace of our seventeenth president, Andrew Johnson. The two trainees we took with us were Dustin Pari and Jen Rossi.

Dustin had worked for a number of local TV stations as a cameraman, so he would be a big help to us in our video work. However, he was still a babe in the woods when it came to investigations. Jen, on the other hand, had been with the group for a while but had never handled the equipment. For both of them, this was an opportunity to take on additional responsibilities.

We put Andy in charge of the training program. After all, he was more than just an experienced investigator. He was someone Grant and I had trained, so he knew exactly what to pass on to Dustin and Jen.

One thing we learned about Dustin on the way down was that he spent fifteen minutes a day arranging his hair. I don't know what he put in it—some kind of mousse, I guess—but it looked like it would go up at the first sign of a spark. I dubbed him unquestionably "the most flammable member of T.A.P.S."

When we arrived in Raleigh, North Carolina, we were greeted by Jim Hall and Dave Gurney, who head up Haunted North Carolina. Their group had joined T.A.P.S.' extended family a couple of years earlier. Like us, they took a scientific approach to the paranormal.

Since we were all hungry and we weren't supposed to reach our destination for another hour, we stopped for dinner at a local restaurant. While we chowed down on Buffalo chicken, we discussed the upcoming investigation. Jim and Dave were going to take part in it so they could learn from us and vica versa. Also, their familiarity with Mordecai House promised to make the evening that much easier for us.

After dinner, we pulled up to Mordecai House and were welcomed by museum educator Chandra Millikin. She showed us around the place, starting with the parlor. The piano there was known to play when tour groups were in the house, even though no one was playing it.

Most of Millikin's experiences had occurred in the bathroom. One time she'd felt her hair lift off her head. When we asked if there was any evidence of Andrew Johnson on the property, she took us to the place where he was born—a separate building still furnished in the manner of the early 1800s.

Millikin said she had felt a distinctly male presence there, and an implicit command to "Get out!" She hoped that we could shed some light on it. We assured her that we would do our best.

Under Andy's guidance, Dustin and Jen used the EMF detector to check the place out. "First," he told them, "get a baseline reading." Then they could examine the rest of the room and have a basis for comparison.

For Dustin, this work was the culmination of something that had begun a long time ago. When he was seven or eight years old, he woke up to see a shadowy figure hovering by the side of his bed. Soon afterward, it happened again. But even at that age, he made a stand. He told the apparition it wasn't welcome there, and it dissipated.

Jen hadn't had any such experiences, but she was eager to become a more integral part of our investigation team. Unfortunately, we hadn't gotten far into the evening before she told us that she felt nauseated. In fact, she had been queasy since dinner. Though she was disappointed, she was unable to continue with the training session.

After Jen left, Jim and Dave told us they had arranged a treat for us—a chance to investigate a haunted battleship in the area. Were we up for it? You bet we were.

But we had an investigation at hand. Though Jen was

on her way back to our hotel, we still had business there at Mordecai House. That came first.

Until Dave announced that he didn't feel well either. He told us that he had been battling a cold for days. With two people down, we decided to scrap the training mission and let everybody get some rest.

It turned out to be a good decision. Before we were done packing up, Grant fell victim to stomach cramps. And later that night, I had the same problem. As it turned out, we had food poisoning—all four of us.

It was bound to happen. We were on the road so often, eating at greasy spoons and worse, it was a miracle we hadn't been poisoned before. I was just glad it happened on a training mission and not in a place we would never have access to again.

Besides, we had a bigger investigation ahead of us—the USS *North Carolina*.

GRANT'S TAKE

Despite the problems we had in Mordecai House, it was great to work with Dave Gurney and Jim Hall. We've met a lot of ghost hunters over the years, but they're a couple of the best, and they run their organization, Haunted North Carolina, a lot like we run T.A.P.S.—basing everything on hard data.

GHOST SHIP
MARCH 2005

T.A.P.S. has investigated some pretty impressive places, but the World War II battleship USS *North Carolina* was still a heck of a challenge for us. Not only was it five hundred feet long but it also went down four decks—and unlike some other places, there weren't any elevators. Depending on how deep you were in the bowels of the ship, you might need forty-five minutes to find your way out.

The guy who met us at the *North Carolina* was Danny Bradshaw, the night watchman, who spends six out of seven nights a week on the 35,000-ton ship. He told us he had seen a ghost on board on three separate occasions.

The first time, a porthole curtain moved aside and a face stared out at him. Then the curtain shut. The second time, his television cut out and an apparition appeared—a figure with a blank look on its face and white flame on its head instead of hair. The third time, Bradshaw was in the mess hall when he felt a hand on his shoulder. He turned, wondering what had gotten hold of him, and saw something human-human-looking standing next to him, the light shining right through it.

Bradshaw screamed. And the human-looking thing made a face, as if to say, "Don't do that." Then it disappeared.

Bradshaw was confident that he had seen something supernatural. However, he needed proof of it. That was where we came in.

Because of the size of the place, we had set aside two nights for the investigation. Even then we would only be able to hit the areas of reported activity. To really give the ship a thorough going-over would have taken weeks.

Our plumbing background often comes in handy in investigations of the paranormal. This case was no exception. Before we descended four stories into parts of the ship no one had visited for years, we scouted each descent with a Roto-Rooter camera. Normally, we snake it down into drain lines to look for breaks. In the *North Carolina,* we used it to look for missing steps and other dangerous conditions.

Shortly after that, I gave the order to "go dark"—in other words, to turn off the lights. Unfortunately, the power for our equipment went off too. The only way to darken that section of the ship and still have juice for our makeshift command center was to unscrew all the lightbulbs in the vicinity.

While Jen kept an eye on all our camera positions from our command center, Steve, Dustin, and Dave went to explore the crew library. Normally, we have to take into account power line activity, appliances, and so on when we conduct an EMF sweep, but not this time. With the power off in that section, those guys were working with a baseline of zero, which made it all the more surprising when they got some EMF spikes.

Grant and I took the opportunity to just wander through the ship, with no particular destination in mind. It was like running an obstacle course with all the pipes jutting out and all the dark, yawning openings in the floor. My father-in-law spent a number of years on a naval ship; I didn't envy him in the least.

Back in the crew library, the temperature was starting to drop. Not only was it evident on our instruments but our team could feel it as well. Dustin identified one corner in particular that was getting colder than the others.

We didn't find anything else that night. After a while, we called it quits. But we weren't disappointed. We still had another night ahead of us.

The following evening, we had the benefit of having all our wires and equipment in place already, so we were able to start investigating as soon as we arrived. The night before, we had focused on the aft part of the ship. This time, we were going to concentrate on the bow.

Steve and Andy made their objective the starboard lavatory, where an enemy torpedo had ripped through the hull. Unfortunately, crewmen had been using the shower at the time. I can't even imagine what it was like to die that way.

Of course, the lavatory was three decks down into a hellhole of dark, creaking metal. Steve is afraid of heights, but he reminded himself that he was going down, not up. As long as he kept that distinction in mind, he was okay.

Remember that scene in *Star Wars* when Luke Skywalker, Princess Leia, and Han Solo fall into a garbage compactor? That's what Andy and Steve felt like with all those stained metal walls around them. Except, luckily for them, the walls didn't start closing in, and there wasn't a hungry alien trying to drag them under.

Finally, they reached the lavatory and the adjoining shower room. In scanning it with his EMF detector, Andy encountered a spike of 2.2. It was quite a number, considering the fact that the power was off. A baseline reading in that area would have been 1.0.

At the same time, Dustin, Dave, and Jim were checking out the mess hall. They had been down there only a few minutes when they heard a crash and looked at each other. Where had it come from? No one knew. They tried dropping lids on pots and jostling the other cookware, but they couldn't produce the same kind of sound.

Grant and I were wandering through the ship again, exploring corridors untouched since the 1950s. At one point, we heard a bang. It sounded pretty close to us—within ten feet, maybe. I couldn't see anyone, but I had a feeling we had become the butts of a practical joke.

Turning to our cameraman, who was right behind us, I asked him if one of our people was down there screwing around. The cameraman swore that we were alone. Frowning, we moved on—and heard the banging sound over and over again.

It sounded as if someone was throwing things at us. We could hear footsteps as well, and voices. But we didn't see anyone. "I'll be pissed if someone's down here," I said, loud enough for a prankster to hear me. A moment later, we stumbled on the ship's brig.

We could hear the *North Carolina* groan like a wounded whale, as if the brig was a place it would rather have forgotten. Had something happened there? Was that why we kept hearing the banging?

As I asked myself the question, a portal closed behind us—just like that. A moment later, I saw a shadow up ahead. Grant saw it too. We pursued it through the long, echoing darkness of the corridor until we saw it duck inside a room.

Okay, I thought, now we've got you.

It took us a few seconds to reach the place. Triumphantly, I swung inside—only to find that the room was empty. Whatever we had seen was gone.

It didn't seem possible. There was only one way in or out of the room, and I was blocking it. I turned to Grant and shrugged my shoulders.

We were lost, cold, and uncomfortable. It was time to call it a night.

To the chagrin of Steve and Andy, our motel accommodations in Raleigh were a little cramped for the purpose of data analysis. They had to share one little table. Still, they rolled up their sleeves and got to work.

Despite their dedication, only one piece of evidence presented itself to them. As they went over the footage from the infrared camera we had placed on the bow, they could see the camera move up and down a couple of times and then fix itself again. It was as if someone had played with it, but all our people had been inside the ship.

Steve and Andy were almost finished when Jim showed up with an audio recording of the time he'd spent with Dustin in the brig. When they played it, they could hear Jim say something and then someone else's response. They assumed it was Dustin speaking—but it wasn't. It was an EVP.

When they played it for Grant and me, we thought we heard the second voice say, "the ship" or "long ship." Where had the voice come from? None of us could say.

On our return to the ship, we met Captain David Scheu, a retired naval officer. He had come to sit with Bradshaw and hear our verdict on the *North Carolina*. Was it haunted or not? That was the expression on his face.

We said that we had experienced and documented activity on the ship. First, we had recorded EMF spikes up to 2.2 in the vicinity of the showers. Second, Grant and I had heard objects crashing near us and seen a shadow that had looked vaguely human. Third, our infrared camera had moved up and down without any of our people moving it. And fourth, we had picked up the EVP in the brig.

We had to conclude that something was going on— something supernatural, though that was all we could say for now. Bradshaw seemed happy that he had gotten some corroboration of his experiences. He no longer had to wonder if he was crazy.

We were happy too. We had gone where few paranormal investigators get to tread. And for Dustin and Jen, who had been disappointed earlier, it was an exceptional training experience.

GRANT'S TAKE

That battleship was enormous. It was like an apartment building that went down instead of up. We could have spent a week there and still not have investigated every last dark nook and cranny.

A CHILD'S FEAR
APRIL 2005

When six-year-old Zach Tanguay told his parents, Denise and Joseph, that his bed shook at night, it was understandably a matter of some concern to them. When he told them that something was yanking at his feet and poking him in the head, their concern grew by leaps and bounds.

Then Denise started having experiences as well. When she went down to her basement-level laundry room, she felt sick to her stomach. Her husband checked out the situation and felt sick as well, yet there was no smell to which they could attribute the feeling.

The last straw was when Denise woke one night to see a bunch of swirling red lights. As she watched, spellbound, in her bed, the lights coalesced into a face. When she shook her husband awake, the face vanished. But after that night, she couldn't go to sleep for fear of the face returning.

Desperate for help, the Tanguays called T.A.P.S. Grant and I put together a small team this time, including Steve, Andy, and Kristyn Gartland, because we were going to work while the boy was sleeping and we didn't want to be too obtrusive.

Kristyn's son had had an experience a lot like Zach's, though he was younger at the time. Because we were able to help him with it, she wound up joining our group. Now she had an opportunity to do for the Tanguays what we had done for her family.

Normally, Grant and I didn't have to worry about Steve during an investigation. He would do his job so smoothly and inconspicuously that he was almost invisible. This time, it was different. With Brian gone, we had promoted Steve to tech manager. We knew he was capable of rising to the occasion, but we would keep an eye on him just to make sure.

When we arrived at the Tanguays' house in Springfield, Massachusetts, Denise was distraught. Zach, on the other hand, was too distracted by video games to exhibit any real anxiety. While Kristyn sat down to speak with Denise, the rest of us looked around the house.

Being parents ourselves, Grant and I are always especially eager to help children. We were going to do anything in our power to get Zach past his problem. We assured him of that.

Between the Tanguays' bedroom, Zach's bedroom, and the laundry room, Steve set up five cameras. Also, Andy put a carbon monoxide detector in the laundry room. He had a suspicion that the Tanguays' experiences there might be attributable to a mild case of carbon monoxide poisoning.

Pretty soon, Zach went to bed and fell asleep. At 10:35, we turned off the lights, and Grant and I went down to the laundry room with an EMF detector. We wanted to get a sense of the magnetic fields down there.

There was plenty of EMF activity. However, that was to be expected, considering the proximity of electrical lines and major appliances. As Grant likes to point out, any consistently high EMF reading is man-made. What we were looking for were spikes and dips.

We didn't find any. Pulling up a couple of chairs, we kicked back. After all, we might have to be there for some time. I smiled at Grant and said, with my usual polish and sensitivity, "Whoever vomits, loses."

He chuckled. "You're on."

Eventually, the discussion turned to Brian and the circumstances under which he had left T.A.P.S. He had been with us for so long that it felt funny doing investigations without him. I was sure he was going to reappear some day and ask for his old job. But after what we had gone through, I couldn't see taking him back. I just didn't think I could deal with him anymore.

Steve, meanwhile, had left the van, where he'd been monitoring the various cameras he had set up. He tiptoed into Zach's room with an EMF detector and managed to take readings around the boy's bed without waking him, no easy feat considering how restlessly Zach slept. But there was nothing unusual to record—just a steady baseline level.

By 1:30, we had gotten everything we could. We packed up and promised to call the Tanguays as soon as we went over the footage. When we left, Zach was moving restlessly but was still asleep.

Steve and Andy spent the next day going over the data. When they were done, they called Grant and me, and we sat down with them. They showed us the video recording of the laundry room when Grant and I had been sitting down there. At one point, we could see a flash of light, but it looked like a reflection off the water heater.

"What else?" I asked.

Unfortunately, they didn't have anything else.

As we had promised, we called the Tanguays and arranged a meeting. We had to tell them that we hadn't found any evidence of the paranormal in their house. We also hadn't detected any carbon monoxide in the laundry room. However, the high EMF readings there might have had something to do with their nausea.

As for Zach's experiences at night, we showed the Tanguays a few minutes of video that we had taken in their son's room. Even over that short span, he had tossed and turned several times. Obviously, he was a restless sleeper.

As we were setting up our cameras, we noticed that the boy played his video games pretty close to the TV screen. Research shows that the part of the brain that responds to video games stays active for a long time. With that in mind, we recommended that Zach end his gaming earlier in the evening.

The Tanguays thought that made sense. They said they had instituted a quiet time during which they read Zach a story, but maybe it wasn't long enough. From that point on, they would see to it he was relaxed before he hit the sack.

We couldn't tell the Tanguays for certain that their house

wasn't haunted. However, our lack of findings seemed to be a relief to them. Denise said she might finally get some sleep.

The only question that remained was how Steve had done on his first night as Brian's replacement. In general, Grant and I were pleased.

We looked forward to working with our new tech manager for a long time.

GRANT'S TAKE

People may think we're disappointed when we don't find a ghost, but that's not true. Jason and I get as much satisfaction from debunking a claim as we do from finding evidence to support one. That's where we part company with many other ghost-hunting groups.

THE HAUNTED MANSION
MAY 2005

We have often heard the cautionary saying "Money can't buy happiness." Maybe so, but I would sure like the chance to find out.

It's hard to imagine my biggest problem being which company to invest in, or which charity to endow, or what to wear at the next blueblood social gathering. It would sure beat worrying about the next payment on the house, or how I'm going to finance five separate college educations.

On the other hand, there's the tale of John Jacob Astor IV, heir to the nation's most amazing fortune back in the early 1900s. His grandfather and namesake, the first John Jacob Astor, had become the richest man in America by investing first in the fur trade and then in Manhattan real estate. John Jacob IV inherited John Jacob's money but not his impeccable sense of timing.

In 1911, John Jacob IV divorced his first wife and, without blinking, married eighteen-year-old Madeline Talmadge Force, a woman thirty years his junior. The wedding, which took place in Beechwood, the Astors' magnificent Newport, Rhode Island, mansion, instantly created an international scandal. The couple went to Egypt for their honeymoon, hoping to stay until the controversy boiled over.

However, Madeline became pregnant a few months later. Wanting the child to be born in the United States, the Astors booked passage back to New York on a spanking-new luxury vessel called *Titanic*. Not a good move, as we in the twenty-first century know all too well.

When the *Titanic* hit an iceberg and started to sink, Madeline got into a lifeboat and survived. John Jacob IV, the richest guy aboard, was forced to go down with the ship. His body was later found and returned to the United States for burial.

It's said that his spirit haunts the ballroom at Beechwood, the place of his greatest joy. Purchased by the Astors in 1881, the mansion was the social hub of New York society for most of what historians call the Gilded Age. But over the last hundred years, it has developed a different kind of reputation—as a place infested with supernatural entities.

The other tragedy associated with Beechwood was the death of a telephone repairman in 1911, a year before the sinking of the *Titanic*. Mixing up his wires, he accidentally electrocuted himself. Now his spirit is said to haunt the basement, whispering of his pain to anyone who goes down there.

Strangely enough, the apparition people have claimed to see at Beechwood is neither John Jacob IV nor the repairman. It's a lady in yellow who's been spotted on and around the mansion's spiral staircase. When anyone approaches her, she disappears.

The only people who live at Beechwood now are its tour guides. However, they were uneasy enough about the goings-on in the place to call T.A.P.S. Our job was to find proof the place was haunted or set the guides' minds at ease.

Grant and I took four investigators with us this time: Carl, Steve, Andy, and Dustin. After all, Beechwood was a big place, and we wanted to be thorough. We were met at the door by Patrick Grimes, the mansion's executive director, who in turn introduced us to tour guide Cecilia "CC" Ice.

CC was beside herself. She had heard voices, felt someone's breath on the back of her neck, and even seen a couple of apparitions. She had closed doors and found out moments later that they were open again. She had heard footsteps behind her on the stairs, but when she turned there was no one there. If her claims were accurate, she had a right to be upset.

Morgen Ballett, the mansion coordinator, had experiences to report as well. She said the ballroom always felt cold to her, even on warm summer days. On more than one occasion, she had turned in response to a voice only to find she was alone.

We set up our equipment, mostly in the basement and on the stairs, and then divided into two-man teams. Grant and I went up to a third-floor bedroom where CC and some of the other tour guides had heard voices. We found that the doors there didn't close very well.

In conditions of high humidity, doors tend to swell up,

and Newport was right near the ocean. A good breeze might push the door open, making it possible for someone in the room to hear footsteps or conversations in the hall outside. It seemed to us that this might be the explanation for the guides' experiences.

In the meantime, Andy and Dustin visited the ballroom, which Ballett had said was always cold. Being the canny investigator he is, Andy checked the heating system in the mansion and discovered that it worked on forced hot air. That meant there was ductwork leading into the ballroom.

After a brief search, he found the vent that was supposed to keep the room warm. For some reason, it was stuffed with rags. The same was true of the vent at the other end of the ductwork, near the furnace. If the ballroom was cold, the mansion's residents had to look no further than those rags.

Over the next several hours, we took a lot of footage in the mansion but didn't run into anything that could be called paranormal. Eventually, we packed up our vehicles and made the drive back to Warwick. It was only about thirty miles, but at that hour there's no such thing as a short trip.

Back at headquarters, Steve and Andy went over the data we had collected. Even under the best of circumstances, this is tedious work. Guys get up to take breaks and get something to eat, but there's no easy way to do this part of the job—and no way to do the job without it.

At one point, they came across what looked like orbs. However, they wound up being nothing more than dust. In the end, there was nothing to report.

However, we had debunked some of the claims at the mansion. And when we presented our findings, we were able to set the tour guides' minds at ease. If we helped someone, it was worth the effort.

GRANT'S TAKE

Though we didn't find any solid documentation at the Astors' mansion, the place did have a feeling of sadness about it. John Jacob Astor IV would have been one of the most powerful men in the world if he had survived his ocean voyage. Unfortunately, he met his match on the *Titanic*.

THE FACE IN THE BATHROOM MIRROR
MAY 2005

Usually, the calls we get are from people who are having paranormal experiences. Occasionally, we hear from other investigators who are in over their heads. That's what happened in Roselle Park, New Jersey.

Dave Tango and Ray Mennincucci had founded Central Jersey Paranormal seven months earlier because of a mutual interest in supernatural occurrences. They had been clipping along just fine, gaining experience and know-how, until they ran into a case of a schoolteacher who believed the sanctity of her house was being violated—either by a ghost or a prankster, she didn't know which.

Dave and Ray could have kept the case to themselves. Some groups out there would have done just that, thinking of themselves instead of their client. But Dave and Ray knew how troubled the homeowner was and didn't want to shortchange her. That's why they called in T.A.P.S.

Grant and I went down to meet them, bringing along Steve, Andy, Dustin, and Paula Donovan. We got together with Dave and Ray in a motel in Newark, New Jersey, and listened to what they had already learned.

Apparently, the homeowner had repeatedly heard objects knocked over and moved on the second floor of her house. Also, an impression like a face print had appeared on her bathroom mirror while she was in the shower. A chair in her computer room seemed to have a life of its own, the basement smelled like perfume sometimes, and she had felt a traveling cold spot.

As far as she knew, the previous homeowner hadn't had any of these experiences, but that didn't make her feel any better. She was so distraught that she was ready to sell her house and move.

After we interviewed her and told her we would do what we could, we started to set up our equipment. Unfortunately, Steve—who never makes mistakes—made one that time by forgetting the power supply to the DVR monitor. I get angry about stuff like that, but I didn't have the heart to give Steve a hard time, especially because he was so upfront about it. If a guy gives you excuses, you want to set him straight. But if he tells you the truth, you're more inclined to let him slide.

Anyway, the rest of the setup went smoothly, giving Dave and Ray an education. They had seen us work on *Ghost Hunters,* but it was different in person. There's a lot of detail work in an investigation that we can't show on television. We just don't have time.

We had Andy, who's great at debunking strategies, take a look at our client's bathroom mirror. He decided to spray cooking oil on the mirror, reasoning that if an image was going to show up, it would do so in cooking oil as easily as in water vapor.

Meanwhile, Grant and I grabbed our thermal-imaging camera and took a walk around the main floor of the house, allowing Dave and Ray to tag along. We hadn't gone far before we heard noises above us that sounded like people walking around. Our first thought was that one of our teams was up there, but that wasn't the case. And when we investigated, we didn't find anyone. One other thing: when we were recording the noises, Grant's laptop seemed to crash. It was all right again a moment later, but we were never able to make a record of what we had heard. A coincidence? Maybe.

In order to give Dave and Ray as varied a learning experience as possible, the next thing we did was split them up and assign them to Steve and Dustin. Dustin mentioned to Dave that he had been terrorized as a child by an entity he couldn't identity. That was what had spurred him to buy some basic equipment and start ghost-hunting.

At the same time, Grant and I went to check out another complaint: that the client's motion sensor alarm in her basement would go off, indicating activity there. We fooled around with the alarm, trying to see if there was a short in the line or something—and got some activity all right. Too bad it was the kind that came with dark blue uniforms in a patrol car. By accident, we had set off the alarm and brought the police!

Still, we were able to find a plausible explanation for the

alarms' going off in the basement. The homeowner had hung some icicle-style Christmas lights down there, and her forced-air heating system would set the lights swaying every time it came on.

By the time we packed up in the wee hours, I was of two minds. But then, it had been a very mixed investigation. We had debunked the activity in the basement, so we could put the client's mind to ease on that count. That was good. However, we hadn't been able to coax a face to appear on the bathroom mirror or get the chair in the computer room to move, so we couldn't shed any light on either of those situations.

As for the footsteps we had heard where there shouldn't have been any . . . that was both good and bad. It was bad because it meant there might be a supernatural presence in the house but good because there weren't any intruders.

I wished that we had been able to produce a record of those footsteps. Unfortunately, they had been lost with the temporary crash in Grant's computer. Or so I thought—until Steve discovered the audio on his DVR disc, recorded in our mobile command unit!

The question was how our client would react to what we had learned. As always, there was one way to find out. As soon as we could, we went back to her house and presented her with our findings.

When we played our recording of the footsteps, she nodded and confirmed that was what she had heard. We explained to her that any repetitive noise or image falls under the category of a residual haunting—one that's like a movie, playing over and over again when the conditions are right. It wasn't going to hurt her.

She seemed more at ease when we told her that. Also, she had gotten some validation of her experiences, so she knew she wasn't crazy. Before we left, we assured her that Dave and Ray would be around if she needed them. That seemed to make her feel good too.

You may wonder why I didn't refer to our client in this case by name. Anyone who saw her on our television show knows that she preferred to remain anonymous. We understand that perfectly. People's careers can be hurt if they're associated with ghost hunting. That's sad, but it's the way it is.

We're just grateful the client brought us into her home. The fact that she was willing to tell her story, if only from the shadows, helps our field immensely.

The next day, Grant and I were working our day job with Roto-Rooter when the subject of Dave Tango came up. Both of us had taken an instant liking to him and the workmanlike way in which he had approached the investigation.

"He's like Brian without all the bull crap," I noted.

In fact, we were looking for a replacement for Brian. Unfortunately, Dave lived too far away to be a full-fledged member of T.A.P.S. But we agreed that if the opportunity arose, we would work with him again.

We just didn't know how soon that would be.

GRANT'S TAKE

Y ou might wonder how a supernatural presence could cause a computer to crash. Remember, ghosts draw on energy in order to manifest. If they can't find it anywhere else, they can pull it out of a computer battery, causing the device dependent on that battery to skip a beat.

PUSHING THEM OUT
MAY 2005

The Worthington family had been in their house for a year, and they didn't want to stay one more minute. The kids, especially, had had it with the place. Fourteen-year-old Josh claimed he had been slapped in the face by an unseen presence while listening to CDs in his room. His sixteen-year-old brother, Nathan, had felt a presence standing next to his drum set and couldn't sleep as a result. And their mother, Cheryl, had sensed something watching her in her bedroom.

Cheryl's two daughters, who were younger than their brothers, had seen dishes fall and heard voices telling them to "get out." Once, they saw what looked like a man standing outside the bathroom.

The family felt especially vulnerable because Cheryl's husband worked nights. They wanted to know what was going on in the house they had been so eager to buy, a vintage structure built back in 1890.

Mike Dion, a member of the extended T.A.P.S. family, had investigated the place previously. His people had felt the touch of something they couldn't see, but they hadn't turned up any concrete evidence of a haunting. However, Mike felt the family's accounts were credible enough to warrant a reinvestigation.

So there we were in Keene, New Hampshire, following Mike's recommendation. The team, in addition to Grant, Mike, and me, included Dustin, Steve, Andy, and Dave Tango. Shortly after we had said good-bye to Dave in New Jersey, he had called asking to come on another case with us.

This one, we felt, was a good opportunity for him to become more familiar with our methods. A training cruise, if you will. Though Dave was obviously fascinated by the supernatural, he had never had any personal experiences with it. That made him pretty much unique in our group, where nearly everybody could point to something in his or her past.

The first investigator with whom we hooked Dave up was Andy, so he could develop an appreciation for Andy's methodical debunking style. They went to the kitchen to check out the claim that dishes were falling off the counter. As it turned out, the countertop was loose, so we didn't have to look to the supernatural for an explanation.

In the meantime, Grant and I went up to the boys' bedrooms and got comfortable—me in Josh's room and Grant in Nathan's. As much as we discount our feelings when it comes to documenting the paranormal, we don't ignore them. Very often, as my partner will point out, our best tools are our human instincts.

About 11:00, Steve, Mike, and Dave moved into the master bedroom to take some still photos. Dave was taking the shots. Knowing a flash could be disturbing, he announced each one. Steve told him he didn't have to do that. He and Mike knew the flashes were coming.

Steve, Mike, and Dave left the master bedroom to go into the hallway when they heard an exclamation. It had come from Grant. He was standing at the threshold of Nathan's room with a snare drum lying on its side at his feet.

I got there a moment later. "What happened?" I asked my partner.

Grant said he had heard the approach of Steve's team and was leaving the room to meet them when something hit him in the back of the ankle. When he looked down, he saw the snare drum from Nathan's drum set.

G.W. was a bit unnerved. He hadn't detected a temperature change in the room or anything else that might have served as a warning. He had just heard a sliding sound and felt the impact of the drum.

But then, moving objects make me a little crazy too.

Steve and Mike remained in the room to see if they could get something on camera. "Did you knock over the drum?" they asked any spirits that might be in the vicinity. "Are you trapped? Can you make a noise for us?"

They were there only a few minutes before they noticed that their batteries were losing power precipitously. Was an entity trying to manifest in the room? If so, it would need energy, and the juice in their batteries would be a good source of it.

However, nothing manifested.

As seriously as we take our business, we can sometimes get a little loopy staying up all night and creeping around in the dark. It's not unusual for us to play tricks on each other. When there's someone new to the group, those tricks start to look like fraternity initiations.

But then, in the literal sense, we are a fraternity. A brotherhood of ghost hunters.

In this case the new guy was Dave. Steve and Andy saw their opportunity when they found a princess's tiara in one of the girls' rooms. Putting it on Dave's head, they led him to believe it was a headlamp.

He wore it for hours, periodically fumbling around in an attempt to find its "on" switch. Steve and Andy could barely keep a straight face. Finally, Grant and I joined them. What the heck is this? I asked myself as I removed the tiara from Dave's head.

Even in the dark, I could see Dave blush. Turning to Steve, I asked, "Is this professional?" I was trying to sound stern, but inside I had to laugh. That tiara on Dave's head was the silliest thing I had seen in a long time.

About five hours into the investigation, Dustin and Mike entered the master bedroom with an audio recorder. The family had heard sounds there, voices and rumblings, and we needed to check it out. At first, the place was quiet. Then Mike heard a cough, which sounded female to him. "Is that you trying to give us a sign?" he asked.

There were no other sounds.

Shortly after that, we wrapped up. We had to be quiet because the kids were all asleep by then. We assured Cheryl that we would speak to her within the week. As the first hints of dawn appeared on the horizon, we got on the road back to Rhode Island.

This time, it was Steve and Dave who went over the data. After all, Dave had said he wanted to get involved in all aspects of the investigation. But it wasn't just a matter of our helping Dave. Before long, he made a contribution by finding an EVP on one of our audio recordings.

It had taken place in one of the bedrooms, right after Steve and Mike had posed a question. You could hear a female voice saying "... keys ..." or "... kitties ..." On the other hand, we weren't sure where Cheryl had been at the time, so we couldn't say for sure it was a legitimate piece of evidence.

The cough Mike and Dustin had heard would have been a nice piece of documentation as well—except we couldn't find a recording of it. That left us with Grant's experience, a questionable EVP, and an unrecorded sound.

Instead of making the trek back to New Hampshire, we called the Worthingtons from our conference room. Needless to say, Cheryl was eager to hear about our experiences and how we interpreted them. All things considered, we said, it seemed there was some activity in the house but we couldn't prove it.

However, we went on, the family didn't have to let a supernatural entity push them out. By getting together and taking a stand, they could show the spirit who was boss and reclaim their home. Others had done it with lasting effect.

But it sounded like Cheryl was leaning toward leaving. "Why stay?" she asked. "It's not fair to the kids."

Whatever she and her husband finally decided, we sympathized with them. We were parents too.

GRANT'S TAKE

've felt the touch of spirits before. I've seen objects move with my own eyes and even captured their movement on videotape. But that was the first time I had been hit with anything as big as a drum.

THE HOUSE WITH A HISTORY
JUNE 2005

As I've noted, I had a problem with visions when I was in my early twenties. It was a constant source of pain to me in that I wondered if I was losing my mind. I don't know how I would have survived the experience if not for the patience and compassion of a ghost hunter named John Zaffis.

Zaffis steadied me and assured me that I wasn't going nuts. He told me that I was just sensitive to paranormal phenomena. He was the one who suggested I find people with similar problems and that we turn to each other for support. That's how I founded RIPS, and then wound up cofounding T.A.P.S. with my friend Grant.

So, when you come right down to it, I have John Zaffis to thank for my status as a ghost hunter. And it's his example that has allowed me to become a good one. But over the years, Zaffis and I have become more than colleagues in the pursuit of the paranormal. We have become close friends.

That's why I always jump at the chance to include Zaffis on one of T.A.P.S.' ghost-hunting forays. It doesn't happen that often because he's got a load of his own cases, and his approach tends to be different from ours. But on one particular investigation, I really wanted Zaffis to come along.

I first learned about it when Grant and I—in our day jobs as plumbers—were taking out a dishwasher from a fish-and-chips restaurant. We got a call on my cell phone from Donna, who told us we had been invited by Norma Sutcliffe to visit the home she shared with her husband in the northern part of the state. I was jazzed because the place had a history of paranormal occurrences.

Twenty years earlier, a previous owner had allowed it to be investigated by Ed and Lorraine Warren, who had been chasing ghosts since 1952. The Warrens, who claimed to be sensitives, said the activity in the house was off the charts, an eleven on a scale of one to ten. But as always, they went strictly by their feelings. There was nothing scientific about their approach to ghost hunting.

At T.A.P.S., any instincts we might have with regard to the supernatural are just the beginning of our investigation. We don't say a place is haunted unless we have backup in the form of documentation. So we had to take any conclusion reached by the Warren group with a grain of salt.

Which brings me to the reason I wanted to include my friend Zaffis in the case. As it happens, Zaffis is the Warrens' nephew. If we were going to examine the same premises they'd examined, it seemed right to bring him along.

In addition to Zaffis, Grant and I recruited Steve, Dustin,

and Donna to visit the Sutcliffe house with us. It had been built in the mid-1700s, even before the War for Independence, when houses were all made of wood and had lower ceilings than we do today. You couldn't walk in and not feel the history in the place.

Legend has it that the original owner got drunk in his barn one night during a blizzard. At first, he tried to wait it out, but eventually he got too cold and tried to make it back to the house. It wasn't far—less than a hundred feet—but he never made it. He was found the next day lying face-down in the snow, frozen to death.

Previous owners had heard footsteps and voices and seen entities, including gray mists, dark shadows, and so on. They had seen doors open and close on their own. Pretty much the gamut of paranormal activity.

I was eager to hear what kind of experiences the Sutcliffes had had.

Mrs. Sutcliffe took Grant, John, and me to a part of the house where she and her husband had seen a door rattle and shake until he finally opened it. In the study, which was full of books, she showed us a chair that vibrated when her husband sat down in it. Then she escorted us to the master bedroom, where she said the bed had shuddered for a minute or two on several occasions.

Zaffis wanted to check out the study and its vibrating chair. Sitting down in it, he opened himself up to the room, trying to get a sense of the forces at work there. I like to do the same thing, but he's been doing it a lot longer than I have.

Zaffis had his first brush with the paranormal at fifteen, when he encountered an apparition of his grandfather.

From that point on, he couldn't learn enough about ghosts and the way they manifested themselves in our lives. His approach to ghost hunting was a little less scientific than the one Grant and I had adopted, but we valued his sensitivity and experience.

As Zaffis maintained his vigil in the study, Donna and I checked out the master bedroom, where the Sutcliffes claimed their bed had vibrated. While Donna reclined on the bed, I sat in a nearby chair. After a while, I felt it vibrate, if only just a little—at exactly the same time that Zaffis felt his do the same.

Then something else happened. As Donna and I were talking, we heard a door in the room unlatch and open. But when we examined it, we saw it was still closed. We were surprised. It had sounded *exactly* as if it were opening.

I turned the handle and opened the door—and with a shock, saw what looked like someone on the other side. To my relief, it was just a hanging jacket. There was a mattress there too, which made it difficult to get past the door into what looked like a walk-in closet.

When I slipped inside, I saw another door at the closet's far end. As it turned out, the closet connected the master bedroom to a second bedroom. It occurred to me that one of our guys was playing a prank, but everyone except Donna, Zaffis, and me was outside the house.

I called Steve and Dustin in the mobile command center and asked them to rewind their recording of what had happened to Donna and me, as captured by the equipment in the room. When they did so, they could hear the door unlatch, just as we had. They marked that portion of the audio for special attention.

By that time, Steve and Dustin were eager to get some time in the house themselves, so we let them out of the van and unleashed them on the study. As they were walking around the room, Dustin felt something grab and squeeze his hand. Afterward, he felt a coldness there, as if his hand had been bathed in ice.

It's a common side effect of physical contact with a paranormal entity. In Dustin's case the feeling didn't last that long, but it can stay with you a while. Of course, everyone's experience is different.

Steve and Dustin also took readings upstairs in the master bedroom. Like Donna and me, they heard the closet door open. When they checked it out, they found that the door on the opposite end was open—even though they had made a point of closing it a few moments earlier.

Not too much later, I made the decision to pack up. At that point, Grant was in the other bedroom—the one that shared the closet with the master bedroom—sitting on the bed and doing some EVP work. The cameraman who was with him stepped out of the room for a moment, leaving Grant by himself.

After a while, Grant realized that something had changed. Using his iPod for a light source, he saw that the closet door to his right was wide open. He hadn't heard it move, but there it was. So he experienced the door phenomenon as well.

When we were done packing, we said goodnight to Mrs. Sutcliffe and began loading our vehicles. We were halfway done when a bat flew into one of the SUVs. Dustin said he didn't care about the bat—unless, of course, it got caught in his hair.

Later that day, Steve and Dustin began their analysis. The first significant footage they came across revealed what appeared to be an orb in the study. However, on closer inspection it turned out to be a reflection from our camera. Then they found something *really* interesting.

As you'll recall, Donna and I had heard the closet door unlatch in the master bedroom. Then, to our surprise, we had seen that it was still closed. Well, later in the investigation the door *did* open itself, right there on one of our cameras. And not a little—it opened a couple of feet.

Then, still on camera, the door closed. But it wasn't done performing for us. Twenty-two minutes later it opened again, this time all the way. Finally, it closed, locking itself. You could hear the latch plain as day.

There was no one in the room. In fact, our quad footage, which allows us to monitor four cameras at once, showed us we were all eating at the time. So whatever was happening seemed to be doing so without human assistance.

Being my usual skeptical self, I had to wonder if there wasn't a draft coming through the closet from the other end. And even though the Sutcliffes and our T.A.P.S. team were all accounted for, I couldn't completely rule out the notion of human intervention. We needed to get back to the house and take another look.

When we returned to the Sutcliffe residence, Grant and I examined the closet door more closely. I went inside the closet and tried to open the door, but it wasn't easy. There was no way a draft could have done it.

Also, there was a mattress standing on its side in the closet, restricting movement in there. Anyone opening the door from inside the closet would have been forced by the mattress to come into view of our camera. That ruled out "foul play."

When we met with Norma Sutcliffe, we showed her the video of the door and told her about our experiences. Something had happened to each and every one of us in her house. All things considered, Grant and I had to agree that the place was haunted.

GRANT'S TAKE

We subject all of our observations to rigorous tests. In the case of the door in the Sutcliffes' master bedroom, we tried to find a way to open it from inside the closet—and couldn't find one. Only then did we agree that the supernatural might have been involved.

HORROR HOTEL
JUNE 2005

Most groups in search of the paranormal are only too happy to embrace "evidence" when they find it. T.A.P.S. is different. We examine that evidence five ways to Sunday, looking for a way to disprove it—to show that it's attributable to a breeze, or a reflection, or some other normal, everyday phenomenon. And the more spectacular the finding, the more eager we are to find an explanation for it.

It sounds masochistic, I know. But that's how we've established a reputation for credibility. Our first impulse is to debunk even when it's our own findings that we're debunking. In fact, we often go at our own observations *harder* than we go at other people's, because we don't want to put our stamp of approval on them and then see someone else pick them apart.

Of course, there are times when we *can't* debunk a finding, when the evidence is so clear that we have to accept it as evidence of the paranormal—which brings us to Eureka Springs, Arkansas, home of the infamous Crescent Hotel.

The Crescent Hotel and Spa was built in 1886 by investors who believed the hot springs in the area possessed healing powers. Its first house physician was a man named Dr. Ellis, a respected doctor in his day. For a long time, the Crescent was known as America's most luxurious hotel.

Then time passed it by, and people began to catch on that the hot springs were just hot springs. Shortly after 1900, the building became a conservatory for young ladies, and it stayed that way pretty much until the 1930s, when a quack named Norman Baker, who claimed to be a doctor, conned people into thinking he had developed a cure for cancer.

That was when things got ugly. Taking the life savings of desperate cancer patients, Baker subjected them to cruel and outlandish methods that had no chance of working. One of his favorite techniques was to open a person's skull, treat the brain with a paste of mashed walnuts and mineral oil, then close the skull up again. In the end, his patients all died, some of them in terrible pain without the benefit of anesthesia.

T.A.P.S. responded to an invitation to check out the hotel with a team of six—Steve, Donna, Dustin, and Dave Tango in addition to Grant and me. We were greeted by Jack Moyer, the hotel's general manager, as well as Ken Fugate, Eureka Springs' resident historian.

The first thing they showed us was the dining room, where a table in the corner was set for two—a Victorian gentleman known as Jacob and the lady he loved, who was supposed to have met him for breakfast in the hotel but never showed up.

Our next destination was room 212, where the esteemed Dr. Ellis had had his offices. Guests of the hotel had reported seeing a man in Victorian dress come out of the elevator, cross the hall, and go straight through the door of room 212—without opening it. In room 419, guests had woken in the morning to find their clothes packed and their bags neatly stacked by the door.

Down in the morgue, where Norman Baker carried out autopsies, the table he used was still standing against the wall. It was in that same room that he'd stored human body parts in large glass jars full of formaldehyde.

The paranormal activity in that area, according to Fugate, was attributable to the guard, who had a hostile nature. Moyer said that any number of guests and employees had had experiences in the hotel, but he wanted T.A.P.S. to document them.

Whenever we can, we stay up late the night before an investigation in order to acclimate ourselves to working into the wee hours. That's what we did our first night in Eureka Springs, finally going to bed at four-thirty or five in the morning.

Sometime later, I heard someone knocking on my door. When I looked at the clock, I saw that it was 5:30. Too fuzzy to figure out what was going on, I said, "Who is it?" A voice outside said, "The building's on fire. You've got to leave."

I put on my clothes and opened the door. There was no sign of a fire—just a little old man going about two miles an hour, knocking on doors. I didn't believe the hotel was on fire, not at the pace this guy was going. Still, I went outside and saw everyone else out there, and realized there was a fire all right.

It was the roof. Apparently, it had been hit by lightning. But like the little old man, no one seemed in any particular hurry. Not even the fire department, when it finally showed up. For a while, I had to wonder if we were still going to be able to investigate the place, or if we were going to have to call it off. Or maybe be restricted in terms of where we could set up.

Fortunately, the damage was minimal and we weren't restricted at all—not that it was going to be an easy job. For one thing, the place was huge. For another, the rooms we were going to check out offered logistical problems. Knowing this, Grant and I had given Donna a list of everything we wanted to cover.

But when she met with Steve, Dustin, and Dave, it became obvious that she couldn't answer their questions—for instance, how to get a cord all the way down into the morgue and where to aim our cameras.

It was Steve who pointed out that we needed to give the rest of the team better information. Grant and I agreed that we would take Steve on the tour next, so he could get a better understanding of the job at hand.

The first inkling we got that there was genuine activity in the hotel was when Dustin tried to get into room 419, where Grant had left his laptop, and felt resistance against the door. Pushing against it, he heard a thump.

It was the laptop. Although Grant had left it on the other side of the room, in front of the TV, it had somehow gotten propped up against the base of the door—even though *there was no one in the room*. Putting the laptop back in front of the television, Dustin made a mental note to tell Grant and me about the incident.

When we heard about it, we immediately made an EMF sweep of the room. It didn't reveal anything out of the ordinary. However, it was a promising beginning. Encouraged, Grant and I took our new favorite toy—our thermal-imaging camera—and went to check out the morgue.

It was eerie down there. Even without the jars full of human body parts, we had no trouble remembering how many corpses had lain in that room, victims of Norman Baker as much as their own cancers.

The camera didn't show us anything as we scanned the morgue table. Everything seemed to be more or less the same temperature, the same energy level, so it appeared pretty much the same color in the viewfinder.

We checked our watches—which showed us it was a few minutes after one—and kept going. In a back room of the morgue, we found a series of numbered lockers. Grant was scanning them when he came across something. Something *incredible,* judging by the look on his face.

He rewound the camera and showed it to me. It was clearly and unmistakably the figure of a man rendered in gaudy thermal colors, less than six feet from Grant and the camera. And the figure was looking back at Grant, as if it was as curious about him as we were about *it.*

When I saw what my partner had captured, my mouth went dry. We had stumbled on a full-body apparition, the Holy Grail of the ghost-hunting field!

Looking closer, I saw that the apparition had a numeral 2 on its sleeve—or seemed to. Actually, it was the numeral on the locker behind the apparition. But it looked like it was embroidered on the apparition's sleeve, and—for no reason we could figure out—it was burning a bright, fiery red.

Also, the apparition seemed to be wearing a hat of some kind. A Civil War soldier's cap? That was how it looked, but it was hard to tell.

Part of me was jazzed beyond belief. But there was another part that told me to be cautious, to keep my enthusiasm in check. We weren't amateurs on our first jaunt through a cemetery. We had to make sure the apparition wasn't something else before we could put any faith in it.

Maybe it was a reflection of Grant. After all, it was looking back at him the way a reflection would. Putting him back where he was standing when he caught the image of the mysterious figure, we looked for a way the light could have bounced off a locker surface into the camera. We couldn't find one.

We also couldn't figure out why that numeral 2 had glowed so red. On the locker, it was spray painted white, and it was as cool to the touch as the rest of the locker. There wasn't any reason for it to be so hot, yet it had definitely shown up that way in the thermal image.

I should have been ecstatic, but I wasn't. I couldn't allow myself to trust what I had seen. We called Steve down, knowing he would approach the problem with a level head, but he couldn't explain the figure either.

The rest of the night was pretty quiet. But then, given what we had already captured, it was hard to concentrate. By 4:30 we had logged nearly fifty hours of recordings. We decided to pack it up.

Usually, I'm perfectly happy to get my sleep and leave

the analysis phase of the investigation to someone else. This time, while Steve and Dave were going over our footage, Grant and I got up and returned to the morgue.

I wanted to disprove the apparition before someone else did. As it turned out, we couldn't do it. We couldn't find anything to make that numeral 2 heat up, we couldn't make Grant's reflection in a mirror fit the form of that figure, and we couldn't figure out where the hat came from.

Also, we couldn't imagine how Grant's laptop had wound up leaning against the door of room 419. Unless, of course, there was some bona fide paranormal activity in the place. So there you have it.

I don't often find myself saying this about a place, but the Crescent Hotel is haunted.

GRANT'S TAKE

There was a moment when I knew what was in the thermal camera and Jason didn't, and that was a moment of pure delight. First, because I had seen something amazing. And second, because I knew how bowled over Jason would be when *he* saw it.

DOCTOR'S HOUSE
JUNE 2005

While we were down in Eureka Springs, we visited the house of Dr. Ellis, the Crescent Hotel's staff physician back in the 1890s. Filled with handsome, well-preserved Victorian furniture and an amazing collection of antiques, the place was owned by a guy named Carroll Heath, who claimed he was a medium.

Heath had long believed that he shared his house with a number of "unseen friends," including Dr. Ellis himself. When he played the piano in his parlor, he said he could feel a crowd gather around him, attracted by the music. On other occasions, he could hear people walking upstairs.

He had seen a lady in Victorian clothing sitting and reading in the bay window of the master bedroom. And in the wooded hollow across the street, visible from that same

215

bedroom, there had been sightings of ghostly beings and strange animals.

Heath was the twelfth owner of the place. One of his predecessors had had the house exorcised, but—according to Heath—the exorcism hadn't been successful. He was hoping T.A.P.S. could provide documentation.

This time, we took Steve along when Heath gave Grant and me a tour of the place. It allowed the setup to proceed much more smoothly. Grant and I decided we would continue with that approach from then on.

The plan was for Dustin and Dave to walk through the hollow across the street. We would have sent Steve, but he's afraid of spiders. Before Dustin and Dave set out, they sprayed themselves with insect repellent. After all, this was Arkansas, a breeding ground for mosquitoes if there ever was one.

Meanwhile, Steve and Donna turned the lights out in the house and took a walk through it with Heath as their guide. I must say it was good working with him. He had never met us before, but he seemed to fit right in.

Dustin and Dave—who was wearing a headlamp that made him look like a cyborg out of a *Star Trek* episode—spent quite a bit of time in that hollow, dodging flying insects and huge spiders. Finally they came across something substantial, which could have been one of those strange animals Heath mentioned. As luck would have it, it was just a confused and scared-looking deer.

At the same time, Grant and I were making our way around Heath's house. At one point, we heard a distinct bang. Following the sound to what we believed was its source, we found something unexpected—but it wasn't evidence of the paranormal. It was evidence that Steve, our tech guru, had screwed up.

One of our cameras was on the floor, having fallen from the place where he'd taped it up. "Looks like Steve owes us four hundred dollars," I muttered. I hate the idea of losing expensive equipment.

As it turned out, the camera was okay. And according to Grant we were actually better off, since we had a better idea of how durable our cameras were. But then, my partner's always looking on the bright side. To me, every silver lining's got a dark cloud.

Back at the hollow, Dustin and Dave weren't having much luck, headlamp or no headlamp. They ran into a cat to go along with the deer, but that was about it.

While Steve and Donna continued to take readings all around the house, Grant and I invited Heath to sit down with us and demonstrate his medium ability by giving me a personal reading. And since he didn't mind, we would record the whole thing.

Over the years, we've come across any number of people claiming to be mediums or sensitives. Of course, when we tested them, very few had any legitimate affinity for the paranormal. We were eager to see how Heath stacked up.

Again, we put our thermal-imaging device to good use. While Heath gave me a reading, Grant trained the camera on us. I have to say here that Heath wasn't working under the best conditions. In addition to Grant, we had a couple of guys with TV cameras in the room, so it wasn't exactly a private encounter.

Also, I was doing my best to block Heath's efforts. Though I willingly repeated my full name three times, giving him permission to read me, I didn't want my innermost secrets plastered all over national television.

Nonetheless, Heath came up with some interesting stuff. He mentioned a farmhouse in the country and said I had memories of it but had never lived there. Check. He said deceased ancestors came to me when I slept. Check again. He said my wife wasn't especially interested in the paranormal. Double check.

Grant didn't comment, but he did seem eager to get his reading next. He handed me the camera. Then, repeating his full name three times, he gave Heath the go-ahead. Heath told him that he had had a visitation from "the other side," a near-death experience. Grant confirmed it.

It was only after Heath had finished with him that Grant showed me what was in the thermal-imaging camera. Though I hadn't seen anything out of the ordinary when Heath read my partner, Heath's reading of me was a different story. As he proceeded, you could see my face and forehead turning bright red, as if my temperature was suddenly skyrocketing. And Heath? He was what Grant called "a psychedelic show," a riot of every color in the rainbow.

Then it got even stranger. As Heath and I spoke, a thick tendril of red moved out of me and began crossing the space between us. It migrated slowly but unmistakably in Heath's direction. Suddenly, just before it reached him, he gestured with his hand—and unknowingly wiped the tendril away.

Now, the thermal-imaging camera is a new tool in our field, which is why we use it every chance we get. There could have been an explanation for what happened that didn't involve the paranormal—for instance, something about the camera itself—so we called the company that made it and got hold of a tech guy.

He didn't seem especially interested in talking to a couple of ghost hunters, making sure to tell us he didn't believe in the paranormal. He also couldn't explain why the camera had recorded that kind of energy.

When Steve saw the footage, he said, "Maybe it's Heath that's haunted, not his house."

When we returned to Heath's parlor to tell him what we had found, he said his "unseen friends" had been active since we'd left, and were interested in our investigation. Grant and I told him that we hadn't picked up anything significant in the hollow, but we had recorded something interesting in his house.

Then we showed him the thermal-image recording. Needless to say, he was delighted. It validated the fact that he had the ability to draw energy from another person, which is a key to any psychic reading.

We were delighted too. With a full-body apparition and a psychic energy migration in the can, our drive back to Rhode Island was a happy one.

GRANT'S TAKE

Once again, I was in the position of having the thermal-imaging camera in my hands and knowing something Jason didn't. It was pretty exciting. But it would have been even *more* exciting if Heath's reading of me had produced the same results.

ROLLING HILLS ASYLUM
JULY 2005

The Rolling Hills Asylum in Batavia, New York, has been the site of misery, insanity, and the deaths of more than a thousand inmates over the course of its 180-year history. It was a prime place for a haunting if we at T.A.P.S. had ever heard of one.

We were invited to investigate Rolling Hills by Lori Carlson, its owner. But the building had had a tortured history long before she got involved with it. It opened its doors in 1827, offering refuge to the unfortunates of Genesee County, New York. Its original residents included orphans, transients, unwed mothers—anyone who couldn't support and care for himself, including the insane.

New York State had a law back then that if people were homeless, they were automatically wards of the state. As a result, they were taken off the street and thrown into asylums.

There, they were given the chance to grow their food on the hundreds of surrounding acres owned by the county.

However, if the legends can be believed, there were sinister occurrences within the brick walls of the asylum. The people in charge of the place practiced devil worship and black witchcraft, secretly tortured their innocent charges, and made sacrifices of human infants.

By the 1950s, the building had been turned into a nursing home, and it remained that way for about twenty years. Then its residents were moved to a new facility nearby, and Rolling Hills fell into disuse. For two decades it sat empty. Then it was refurbished and reopened as Carriage Village, a collection of small shops. It became Rolling Hills Country Mall in January 2003, a far cry from a house of madness and despair.

But the grimmest features of the place remained intact over the years—for instance, the army of grass-covered mounds that still surrounds it. These are unmarked graves, filled with the bodies of a thousand John and Jane Does.

Inside the building, you can still see the morgue where the bodies were examined prior to burial. Rolling Hills slaughtered its own animals, so it had a large meat locker. When the morgue was full, the administrators used the locker to store additional corpses—or so the story goes.

When we arrived at the place, we were a team of six that included Grant, me, Dustin, Paula Donovan, Steve, and Dave. Carlson and her manager, Jim Swat, came out to welcome us. They were eager to share the list of claims people had made, which included ghostly voices, doors opening and closing on their own, and chairs moving about.

People had smelled strange smells, felt their hair tugged,

and heard noises where there shouldn't have been any. And then there were the apparitions. One person had glimpsed a couple of kids walking through the place. Another had seen a woman being carried by her elbows.

The asylum had had three floors. The first was where its offices had been located. The second was where its doctors had practiced electroshock therapy. On the third floor, we were introduced to a room where teenagers broke in from time to time and performed black magic rituals like those in the old Rolling Hills stories. We're talking candles, weird paintings of cats, bats and skulls on the walls, and pentagrams.

For me, this was something of a homecoming. I had spent the first part of my life about half an hour from Batavia, in a town called Canandaigua. Fortunately, Rolling Hills was nothing like the place where I had grown up.

I was reminded of that as we were setting up our equipment and we spotted a car way off in the distance. It was just sitting there with its lights on, as if watching us and waiting for us to leave, even though our hosts had kept our investigation a secret.

We asked them if they knew anything about the car, and they said they didn't, so we drove over there to see what was going on. Before we could get there, the car sped away. To this day, we don't know who was in it or what he wanted.

In any case, we had an investigation to carry out. Steve and Donna began their part in the basement, where there was a strong and unmistakable smell of feces. Anybody who thinks ghost hunting is a glamorous deal should spend a few minutes down there. As it was, Steve and Donna could barely wait to escape.

Dustin and Dave took the second floor. They weren't getting anything unusual on their instruments, which was leading them to believe that the claims about the place were exaggerated—until Dustin felt something grab his ear.

It wasn't a light brush, either. Not the way he described it to us later. It was a firm, two-fingered tug.

At that point, Grant and I were in the furnace room carrying out a thermal scan. Let me say this without reservation: we love our thermal-imaging device. It opens up ways of looking at the paranormal that we never had access to before.

Unfortunately, we weren't picking up anything with the thermal imager. If there's nothing there, it doesn't matter how sophisticated your equipment is. Then, just like Dustin, I had an experience.

It wasn't a tug on the ear, though. It was more ominous. The furnace door, a metal monstrosity about two inches thick, suddenly swung closed on me.

My first thought was that Grant had closed it on me as a joke, but he denied it. Unsure about what to make of the incident, I pushed the door open. This time, it swung closed even harder, pinning me for a moment.

Okay, I thought, something's going on here. Shoving the door off me again, I took a moment to examine it. As far as I could tell, there was no reason it should have swung anywhere. I tried kicking it, but it didn't move an inch. And yet it had swung closed with no apparent provocation.

Suddenly, it swung open again. And as it did, I heard a hissing sound. The next thing I knew, Grant and I were drowning in a river of flapping bat wings, and I did the one thing no self-respecting ghost hunter should ever do—I yelled.

GRANT'S TAKE

Jason's yell spooked me more than the sudden appearance of the bats. If Jason's scared, I thought in that moment of surprise, I'm dead. Of course, neither of us was in any danger. The bats were more of a nuisance than anything else.

Evil person that I am, the bats gave me an idea. A few minutes later, we found Dave and Dustin. With a straight face, I sent them down to the basement—where, like us, they were swarmed over by a wave of bats. Except in their case it was worse, since Dustin is very particular about his hair. The thought of bats pulling at it made him freak a little.

And we weren't done yet. After all, Steve and Donna hadn't gotten the bat treatment yet. Before long, we heard their yells of surprise and disgust. Mission accomplished, I thought gleefully. In fact they had to brave the bats twice, because they forgot to take their cameras with them when they went running the first time.

We sure had fun that night. But the next day, when we went over our recordings in a nearby Holiday Inn, we were disappointed—both for ourselves and for the owner of Rolling Hills. We couldn't find a shred of evidence to prove the place was haunted.

On the other hand, Dustin had felt a tug on his ear and I had had a furnace door close on me, so there is some sort of activity there. We just weren't lucky enough to document it.

THE WINCHESTER MYSTERY
JULY 2005

The Winchester Mystery House in San Jose, California, was about as weird a place as you can imagine. But then, it hadn't been built according to any plan. For thirty-eight years, seven days a week, twenty-four hours a day, workmen simply added rooms onto what was originally a six-room farmhouse, making it up as they went along.

You see, a psychic back East had told Sarah "Daisy" Winchester that her husband and daughter had been killed by the ghosts of all the Native Americans who had fallen victim to the Winchester rifle, the most famous weapon in the Old West. If Daisy herself didn't want to perish, she had to build a house out West and keep on building. Never mind that it didn't make sense. Daisy fell for it hook, line, and sinker.

Construction stopped when Daisy died of natural causes in

1922 at the age of eighty-three, but not before her house had grown to include 160 rooms. Forty of them were bedrooms. The place also boasted ten thousand windows, forty-seven fireplaces, and forty staircases, most of which led nowhere. Some doors led nowhere as well. As I said, the workers made it up as they went along.

Before the 1906 San Francisco earthquake, Daisy slept in the room still known as the Daisy Bedroom. However, after the quake made part of the structure unstable, she boarded up the Daisy room and thirty others.

The house still exhibits its owner's preoccupation with protecting herself from the malevolence of evil spirits. Spiderweb designs, which she considered good luck, show up over and over again. The same goes for the number thirteen. A chandelier that originally had twelve candle holders was changed so it could hold thirteen candles instead. Clothes hooks around the mansion are also arranged in multiples of thirteen. A stained-glass window boasts thirteen colored stones—and so on.

Over the years since Sarah Winchester's death, all kinds of paranormal activity had been reported in the house. That was why it was on the Top Ten list of sites Grant and I wanted to investigate. You can imagine our excitement when we got a call from Donna saying that we had been asked to go out to San Jose and scour the Mystery House for ghosts.

Grant and I put together a team that included Andy, Steve, Donna, and Dave Tango to make the long drive across country. When we arrived, we were greeted by Cheryl Hamilton, the mansion's marketing coordinator. The first thing she showed us was an array of glass showcases full of Winchester rifles, the weapon of choice in the Old West, from the 1866 model known as Yellow Boy for its brass receiver to the 1892 carbine that John Wayne carried around in his films.

Next, Hamilton took us to the Daisy Bedroom, where guests had felt drastic temperature changes—presumably because Daisy's ghost still inhabited the place. She also showed us the Goofy Staircase, a hundred-foot-long configuration of forty-four steps that took seven turns to go up a total of seven feet.

The Grand Ballroom was big and elegant, its intricately designed parquet floors so well preserved that we had to take off our shoes to walk on it. People in the house had reportedly heard the ballroom's organ playing when there was no one there. On another occasion, a team of workers in one of the basements (the mansion has two!) had spotted a man standing by the boiler dressed in coveralls. When they tried to get a closer look at him, he disappeared.

Because of the way the Mystery House was built, not to mention its sheer size, it was a difficult and stressful setup. Steve got cranky about the fact that Dave and Donna weren't as familiar with the equipment as he was. Then we learned that we would lose power to our instruments as soon as we turned off the lights.

Despite it all, Steve muddled through. He coolly and methodically rerouted our cables to the parts of the house beyond the scope of our investigation, where the power would stay on. Before too long, we were able to go dark and begin ghost hunting.

As one of us commented, it was like walking through Mrs. Winchester's mind. A bizarre place, no question about it. And yet, it was more fun than almost anything else I can think of.

Grant and I started our investigation in the basement, where people had heard odd banging sounds. We heard them as well. However, as plumbers, we had heard such noises before. More than likely, they were the result of a plumbing problem rather than a haunting problem.

Steve and Dave heard banging also, except they were exploring the ballroom. They also ran into a phantom smell there—in other words, one that couldn't be explained. The theory is that spirits express themselves through these smells, though it's seldom easy to figure out what they're saying.

Outside of these experiences, it turned out to be a fairly uneventful investigation. However, we still had our analysis to look forward to. Packing up our equipment, we thanked Cheryl Hamilton and said we would be back.

In this instance, it wasn't just the usual suspects—Andy, Steve, and Dave—going over the data. Donna, who wanted to learn another facet of what we did, pitched in as well. After a while, her head was spinning. It was harder than she had ever imagined.

She gave Steve and the others a lot of credit. But then, that kind of work isn't for everyone. You've got to be a little crazy to spend your entire day in a hotel room staring at a video monitor.

Unfortunately, the team failed to turn up a single piece of verifiable evidence. At that point, it was up to Grant and me to give Cheryl Hamilton the news that we hadn't found anything conclusive. She took the information very much in stride.

We were relieved. After all, you never know how that's going to go. And with only twenty percent of our cases indicating paranormal activity, we end up giving out that kind of report a lot.

Anyway, the Winchester Mystery House was certainly mysterious. It's not hard to see why people think it's haunted.

GRANT'S TAKE

On the one hand, you could say that our visit to the Mystery House was a failure because we didn't find anything of supernatural origin. On the other hand, it was a wonderful opportunity to examine one of the more bizarre artifacts of life on Earth. I'm glad we went, ghosts or no ghosts.

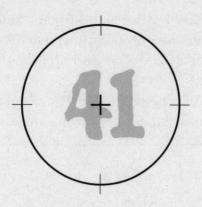

ST. AUGUSTINE LIGHTHOUSE
JANUARY 2006

The St. Augustine Lighthouse was the site of one of our greatest ghost-hunting adventures ever. And yet, we almost overlooked it in our whirlwind tour of St. Augustine, a city on Florida's east coast just south of Jacksonville.

T.A.P.S. was there to investigate what has become known as the most haunted town in Florida, if not the entire United States. In the process, we learned that St. Augustine is the oldest permanent European settlement in North America, preceding the English colony at Jamestown, Virginia, by more than forty years. It was named by the Spanish, who established a garrison there on the Feast Day of St. Augustine in the year 1565, part of their plan to run the French out of the area.

The city is full of haunted restaurants, haunted inns,

and haunted landmarks, like the city gates. There was so much to investigate that we had no intention of looking at a lighthouse. But wherever we went, the locals kept telling us, "Check out the lighthouse! You've *got* to check out the lighthouse!" Finally we decided to take some mopeds over there and see what the fuss was about.

We were glad we did. Even from a distance, the lighthouse's tower sent chills up and down our spines. It had red and white stripes like a gigantic candy cane, but there was nothing sweet about it. You got the feeling there was something creepy going on inside.

The first thing Steve said was, "I can't go up there."

As we have noted already, he has a fear of heights. We make fun of it sometimes, but we also know it's a legitimate phobia. We assured Steve that he wouldn't have to go up into the tower.

We made arrangements to stay and investigate the lighthouse. But as it turned out, there weren't many reports of supernatural activity in the tower. Most of them were in the lighthouse keeper's house, which was more than a hundred feet away.

The day of the investigation, there were six of us representing T.A.P.S.—Grant, me, Dustin, Donna, Steve, and Brian Harnois. Brian had broken up with his girlfriend and had asked to rejoin the group. After much soul-searching, we decided to let him back in, and he hadn't yet given us reason to regret it.

But Brian was no longer our tech manager. Steve had taken over that position and was doing a great job at it. So in effect, Brian was working for Steve now.

The lighthouse's director of education, Paul Wenglowsky, was waiting for us when we arrived. He told us that at 140 feet, St. Augustine is the eighth-tallest lighthouse in the country, and also the oldest in the state of Florida. He also said that it has been the setting for tragedy right from the beginning.

While the lighthouse was being built in the 1870s, its supervisor of construction, a guy named Hezekiah Pity, moved his family down there. Unfortunately, the move was one he would regret. He had set up a handcar-style rail system to get supplies up from the beach, and his kids loved to get in the rail car and ride it down. One day the brakes failed and the car plunged into the ocean, drowning two of Pity's daughters, Mary and Eliza.

People said the girls' spirits lingered in the lighthouse keeper's house, manifesting themselves in the form of voices in the parlor and footsteps running up the stairs. And it wasn't just employees who had heard them. Patrons had experienced them as well.

Some years after the girls' death, one of the lighthouse keepers hanged himself on the front porch of his house. According to reports, his spirit remains there as well. The last keeper, James Pippin, reported that he had heard footsteps and voices, and had seen the lights go on and off on their own. He finally abandoned the place and went to sleep in a little Coast Guard bungalow.

However, most of the activity had been in the basement. The executive director of the lighthouse had been down there one day and saw a man walk past her. When she called out to him, no one answered, and though she looked around she couldn't find anyone there. Others had reported seeing a man in uniform in the same area.

It took us a while to negotiate the 219 steps that spiraled up to the top of the tower. The landing at the halfway point, we were told, had seen some ghostly activity. There was a bucket there full of sand that simulated the weight of the oil the lighthouse keeper would lug up the stairs. Over the years, people had reported hearing the bucket picked up and dropped.

Surprisingly, Steve made it to the top along with the rest of us. But he wouldn't go outside on the catwalk that circled the tower. For once, I didn't give him a hard time. I knew how tough it had been for him to get that far.

We were joined on the catwalk by Allan Studer, a retired lighthouse guide, who told us that every evening the employee in charge of closing the tower would padlock the door up there. But it wasn't unusual for the door to be found open again in the morning, its alarm never having gone off.

People had also seen a woman in white or a little girl in period dress on top of the tower during severe storms. It was hard to picture such a scene considering how blue the sky was at the moment. Still, the image made me shiver a little.

When we set up our equipment, we distributed most of it throughout the lighthouse keeper's house. Our newest toy was a portable Geiger counter developed for us by Ron Milione, our T.A.P.S. tech guy back home. The theory is that supernatural entities emit a radioactive frequency. With a Geiger counter, we had the wherewithal to detect that frequency.

Ghost hunting is a difficult business. You can work at it for years and not record any documentation of your experiences. When it's available, you want to make sure you have the tools to capture it.

We put very little equipment in the tower, because there hadn't been much activity there. One device we did deploy there was a wireless audio unit. It was Brian's job to place it where we could access it from our mobile command center.

He knew that if he placed the unit on a metal surface, he would get reverberation. So he positioned it two-thirds of the way up the stairs on a wooden bench. At that point, he was ready to move on to the next task.

But I wanted the unit all the way up at the top of the tower, so I asked Brian to reposition it. He wasn't happy about climbing back up the stairs again, but he did it. And again, he figured he was through with the job.

Unfortunately, the unit wasn't working. When Grant saw that, he asked Brian to change the battery. Muttering to himself, Brian dragged himself up to the top of the tower again and changed the battery. Then he came back down.

But the reception from the unit was tinny because of the steel surface on which it was sitting. So Brian had to go up again and put it back on the wooden bench where he had left it in the first place. And he didn't complain once, at least not loudly enough for any of us to hear him.

This is why we've kept the guy around for so long. He might have given us ulcers from time to time. He might have made us want to kill him. But when push comes to shove, nobody works harder than Brian Harnois.

Dustin and Steve, meanwhile, were in the basement of the house, checking out claims of voices, footsteps, and apparitions. After Brian joined them, they thought they heard a female voice, and they tried to trace it to its source. Unfortunately, they couldn't figure out where it was coming from.

At that point, Grant and I were in the tower. We had positioned a thermal camera at the bottom shooting up, just to see what we could pick up. Climbing the stairs to the landing, we picked up the sand bucket and dropped it. The sound shot through the tower like the crack of a whip.

Then we checked out a window a few feet away. It turned out that it was held shut by a sandbag. Apparently, it didn't close very well.

Without the sandbag, the window was free to swing with the wind. After a while, it slammed—and then slammed again. Grant and I smiled at each other. The sound of the window slamming was almost exactly the same sound as the bucket dropping. We had debunked our first claim of the night.

We were about to leave the tower when we heard something—the sound of people talking. On the other hand, the conversation might have been an echo of our own. We talked again and listened for an echo, but there wasn't any.

Strange. And it got stranger when we heard a little girl's voice, followed by footsteps. And more conversation. A man and a woman, it seemed to us. Then it sounded like a man and a child, and the child was jabbering something.

The voices seemed to be coming from farther up the tower, so we ascended the stairs. It was then that we saw something walk by a window, blotting out the light—not once, but twice. It looked like the head and shoulders of a man. And it seemed to be moving up the stairs, just as we were.

We started moving up the stairs again, hoping to catch up with whatever we had seen. Then something stopped us cold. It was a human silhouette, not more than ten feet away. And it was leaning over the railing, looking down at us.

We didn't want it to get away. Without thinking, I bolted up the stairs in an attempt to catch up with it. Grant stayed behind with his flashlight in hand, making sure nothing got past me. When you've worked together as long as we have, you can move without hesitation because you know what the other guy's going to do.

I couldn't catch more than a glimpse of the dark figure as I climbed, but I was sure it was navigating the spiral stairs above me. If it was a race, I might not have won it. Lucky for me the tower ended not too much higher up.

Finally, I reached the top—but there was nothing there except a padlocked door. Cursing to myself, I called down to Grant. But he hadn't seen anything go past him. Whatever we were chasing, it had vanished into thin air.

One thing we knew was that we wanted to send Dustin and Brian into the tower to see if they would experience anything like what we had experienced. Having heard what happened, they were more than eager to give it a shot.

"Hello?" they called as they started up the stairs.

Almost immediately, they heard a response. It was unquestionably a female voice, moaning, asking for help. They were still absorbing it when they saw movement on the stairs above them.

Running up the stairs, they saw something grab the handrail and look down at them. Then it seemed to disappear—and reappear a level closer to them. It was as if the thing was coming down, not running away from them. Then they saw a small explosion of light and the figure vanished.

Brian was jazzed beyond belief. What he had experienced made everything worthwhile—all the angst, all the backbreaking work. He had seen almost a full-body apparition, the Mona Lisa of paranormal activity. "I can die a happy man now," he told us.

Grant and I had seen the thing. So had Brian and Dustin. The only one who hadn't was Steve, who had held back from exploring the tower because of his acrophobia. But what we had seen changed his mind. He had to experience it for himself.

It wasn't easy for him to go up those stairs in the dark, all by himself, even with a flashlight in his hand. But he didn't want to be the only one who left the lighthouse empty-handed. After a while, Grant and I decided to join him for support.

It wasn't long before we heard footsteps. A moment later, we caught a glimpse of something—a moving shadow. But it wasn't as close or as distinct as what we had seen before.

"Show us a sign," we asked. "Please."

Just then, we spotted something on the landing above us—a shadow. And we heard noises like the ones Grant and I had heard before. We swept up the stairs, hoping to see the figure again.

But we couldn't find it.

Steve was disappointed. We stayed on the stairs for a while, hoping something would happen. But eventually, we had to call it a day. As we left the tower, I heard Steve mutter to himself, "Damn."

Later that night, when we had a chance to talk with our

TV production crew, we found out they had had experiences as well. Justin Tucker, a production assistant, had seen bright orange light come out of the tower entrance and go off into the trees just after Grant and I entered the lighthouse. Others heard their voices being called several times, but couldn't see who was calling them.

Some of them were so spooked they refused to go back into the lighthouse, even if it cost them their jobs. Kendall Whelpton, the camera operator, felt his headphone removed from one of his ears and heard someone whisper to him. It shook him up so much he needed a moment to regain his equilibrium.

The sound man back in the lighthouse keeper's residence, who was monitoring the audio in the tower, heard the cry for help that Grant and I had heard. It was so clear, so distinct, that he almost dropped his coffee. After that, he wouldn't go near the tower for anything.

Finally, we called it a night, packed up, and took the data we had collected back to our hotel. We're always eager to see what we've unearthed on an investigation. This time, "eager" didn't begin to describe it.

The evidence was everything we could have hoped for. Our video footage clearly showed a shadow at the top of the stair. A moment later, we heard a female voice crying for help, and saw the shadow dart to the right.

It was exactly what Grant and I had witnessed in the tower. Then something or someone peeked over the railing. Had it been a person, a light would have gone off, triggered by the tower's motion sensor. But it remained dark.

We took the video back to the lighthouse and showed it to Wenglowsky, who had always been amused by the lighthouse's reputation but hadn't believed in anything like ghosts. When he saw the footage and heard the call for help, he turned pale. "That lighthouse is haunted," he said.

Grant and I had to agree. However, no one had been hurt by the spirit or spirits residing there, so there wasn't any reason to be afraid of them. As far as we were concerned, they could stay right where they were.

GRANT'S TAKE

As pumped as I was about seeing that apparition, my excitement was tempered by my sympathy for Steve. After all, everyone but him had glimpsed that thing in the lighthouse. But there will be other investigations, and Steve is sure to experience his share of strange occurrences.

THE STANLEY HOTEL
FEBRUARY 2006

That scene from the 1980 movie *The Shining* has become a part of our national consciousness, a relic of Hollywood moviemaking as famous as any other: actor Jack Nicholson, all stubble-faced and disheveled, with an axe held tight in his hands and a murderous glint in his eyes, is seen leering through the bathroom door he has just smashed. With a crazy glee in his voice, Jack's character screams to his intended victims, his terrified wife and son, "Heeeere's JOHNNY!"

It was a familiar phrase among Americans, the one announcer Ed McMahon had used to introduce popular late-night talk show host Johnny Carson since the early 1960s. Hearing it shrieked by a madman who was about to hack up his family was nothing short of horrifying.

Weeks earlier in the film, Nicholson's character—a

failed private-school teacher turned playwright, named Jack Torrance—had moved his family to the Overlook Hotel in Colorado, where he had taken a job as winter caretaker. It was supposed to give him the quiet time he needed to finish his play and maybe salvage his life. Instead he went bug-eyed nuts, influenced by the powerful supernatural forces running rampant in the handsome old hotel.

The film was based on a book by author Stephen King, a name every horror fan should know. But the Overlook Hotel wasn't strictly a child of King's fertile imagination. It was inspired by an actual place—the stately Stanley Hotel in Estes Park, Colorado.

So when Donna sat me and Grant down in our confer-ence room and told us we had been invited to investigate the Stanley Hotel, my partner and I looked at each other and grinned. For two veteran ghost hunters, it was very much a dream come true.

Over the years, guests of the hotel had claimed to see little kids running up and down the hall, even when there weren't any children staying there. Mr. Stanley, the former owner, had reportedly been seen in the lobby and in his favorite room, the Billiard Room. More recently, the police had been called in when a female guest started screaming for no apparent reason.

It was all we could have hoped for and more.

Though it was wintertime, the place wouldn't be shut down entirely, so we would still have to work around a few guests. However, we were assured we wouldn't have any problems in that regard. Unfortunately, Donna had to work and couldn't go on the trip, so we would have to do without her experience and sensitivity. Our team would consist of Grant and myself, Steve, Brian, Dave, and Lisa Dowaliby.

Lisa had come to us a couple of years earlier. She had had some experiences that she couldn't explain and she was still wrestling with them when she saw our show on the Sci Fi Channel. To say she was interested in speaking to us would be an understatement.

As soon as we met Lisa, we realized how valuable she could be to T.A.P.S. She had worked in a veterinarian's office and possessed great organizational skills, and generally knew how to get things done. At the same time, Donna was getting overwhelmed setting up cases, not only for the TV investigations but also for our home group.

So at first we put Lisa to work helping Donna, and she did a bang-up job. She's one of those strong-willed people who can be firm and charming at the same time, so you don't feel you're being coerced into doing what she wants. Later on, she asked to take part in some investigations, and she really flourished in that role.

So there she was, pretty much taking Donna's place in this instance and heading to the airport with us. You could see the excitement on her face. She was determined to make the most of the opportunity.

The next day we found ourselves driving through the Rocky Mountains, talking about the investigation ahead. Apparently, the hotel property was made up of three separate buildings, and activity had been reported in all three. It was winter, so we would experience the same snowy conditions as in the movie.

Because of the size of the place and the promise it held for paranormal investigators, we decided to spend two entire nights there. Fortunately, the management had offered to put us up, so we wouldn't have to go back and forth to a motel. En route through the mountains, we saw elk everywhere. Between the snow, the aspen trees, and the elk, it was like being on another planet.

Finally, we came in sight of our destination. The Stanley Hotel was a big white building with a red roof nestled comfortably in the lap of the Rockies. Billy Ward, the concierge, greeted us as we pulled up. Inviting us in, he told us how the hotel's original owner, F. O. Stanley, had moved to Colorado in 1903 in the hope that the dry mountain air and cool climate would help his tuberculosis.

When Stanley's health improved dramatically, he thought it was so great that he and his wife built a hotel in Estes Park. The place opened in 1909 and was immediately hailed as one of the nicest hotels in the country.

Stanley, as you may know, was one of the two twin brothers who founded the Stanley Motor Carriage Company back in the late 1800s. Their cars were affectionately known as Stanley Steamers because they were powered by steam engines, which were all the rage until the newfangled internal combustion engine became available.

Anyway, by 1909 Stanley was more focused on his hotel than on the car manufacturing business. The place was built with beautiful hardwood floors, ornate wooden moldings, and the fanciest furnishings available at the time.

The first room Ward showed us was the MacGregor Room, which was used to shoot the party scenes in a TV miniseries, also called *The Shining*, that aired in 1997. According to Ward, the hotel's cooks had once heard a party going on in the MacGregor Room—only to find, on leaving the kitchen, that the room was empty. Another time, a manager and another employee were talking in that room when a ghostly figure appeared between them.

"You get an eerie feeling in here," said Ward, "as if people are walking behind you."

He had had a paranormal experience of his own in the hotel. When he was new to the staff and learning to conduct the night audit, he had seen books come flying off a shelf.

Room 217 was the one where Stephen King had stayed on the last day of the season back in 1973. In fact, he and his wife had been the only guests. In the Jack Nicholson version of *The Shining*, 217 had been renumbered 237 so the hotel in which they were shooting the movie, a place called the Timberline Lodge, wouldn't have a problem booking its room 217.

No matter what it was called, the room had a long association with a former maid called Mrs. Wilson. Back in 1911, when she joined the staff of the hotel, it was the maid's job to light acetylene gas lamps in each room. If she did a poor job, she would blow the place up, so she had a lot more responsibility than today's hotel maids.

According to various guests over the years, Mrs. Wilson is still in the room. There are stories that people on their way to the bathroom suddenly see the light go on in there, as if someone was looking out for them. It's believed that Stephen King had an experience with Mrs. Wilson as well. Apparently, he and his wife left their luggage in the room without unpacking it. When they returned forty-five minutes later, they found their clothes in the dresser drawers and their bags stacked neatly in the closet.

Of course, that could have been done by a flesh-and-blood maid. But none of the hotel's staff seemed to know anything about it when King asked them.

As we talked with Ward, we were joined by other employees. Like the concierge, they had stories to tell. Krishanthi Fernando, the night auditor, talked about complaints from guests on the fourth floor that children were playing loudly in the hall outside their doors. When hotel staff investigated, there weren't any kids to be found.

Krishanthi speculated that these children were the ghostly son and daughter of one of the maids who'd worked on the fourth floor. It was her understanding that Stephen King had seen them—a dark-haired boy and a blond girl—and also seen the ball they were throwing back and forth between them.

Ward noted that room 401 was one of the most haunted places in the hotel. One night, he said, a male guest took off his wedding ring and set it on the night table beside his bed. A couple of hours later, he woke to find a man picking up the ring. Before the guest could stop him, the man walked into the closet. But when the guest followed him in, the closet was empty—and he never recovered his ring.

Krishanthi told us about something that had happened just that past season. A married couple was staying in room 412 when, in the middle of the night, the wife started screaming. When Krishanthi came upstairs, she found the woman rolling on the floor and shrieking, "Help me!" at the top of her lungs.

Though nearly incoherent, she was able to communicate a feeling that an energy was trying to take her over—to possess her. Krishanthi and food and beverage director Sandy Murphy walked the woman down the hall, hoping the exercise would snap her out of it. Suddenly, with what Murphy described as "the strength of twelve men," the woman's hands clenched into fists and she sent the hotel employees flying in either direction.

Finally, paramedics arrived and took the woman away in an ambulance. When she arrived at the hospital, she was checked for drugs, but the doctors couldn't find any. Despite her outburst, she was totally clean.

Next, Ward took us to the Manor Hall, a smaller version of the main building. In room 1302 on the Manor Hall's third floor, a housekeeper had just finished tidying up when she saw the head housekeeper out in the hall. After they talked, the head housekeeper poked her head into the room to make sure it was up to snuff. What she saw was a picture of chaos, with bedclothes pulled off the bed and the room's wall hangings strewn across the floor. And yet neither of them had heard a sound.

In fact, Ward told us, every room on the third floor had a problem in that its windows went up and down on their own. Grant and I assured him that we would check them out. Then we followed the concierge out of the Manor Hall and into the hotel's third building, an airy, spacious place called the Concert Hall.

Ward said this structure had sheltered a homeless lady, unbeknownst to hotel management. As the story goes, she snuck into the hall to get warm. However, she made the mistake of hiding in the basement, which was colder than upstairs, and was eventually found frozen to death.

Sometime later, Ward was playing host to four teenaged girls—guests of the hotel—who had gone with him to the Concert Hall to hear ghost stories. Naturally, he told them about the homeless lady. Chills running up and down their spines, they got out their cameras and began to take pictures of the place—until they heard a high-pitched shriek from the side booth, and ran like the dickens.

"I'm not fond of going there after dark," Ward said of the Concert Hall.

One thing we found early on in the investigation was that it was easy—and fun—to give each other static shocks. The air in Colorado was pretty dry, and there were carpets everywhere, so all we had to do to build up a charge was walk around. Then we reached out with our forefingers and touched each other on the ears. One time when I touched Grant's ear I generated a five-inch spark. It was pretty impressive.

GRANT'S TAKE

When I wasn't running around shocking everybody like a little kid, I got to thinking: with all that static in the air, it had to be easier for spirits to manifest. After all, they needed energy to make an appearance. Wasn't static electricity as good as any other kind of energy? It was an interesting question.

The Stanley had everything you could ask for in an investigation: a list of impressive stories, creepy old buildings, and an ominous feeling in the air. But it was too big for us to cover everything we wanted to cover. We decided to focus on a half-dozen of the most active locations.

Grant and I started our night in the ominous-looking MacGregor Room, which we scanned with an audio recorder and a thermal-imaging camera. The camera picked up a trio of rectangular-looking light spots, all moving in unison. Were they reflections or something more meaningful? We would reserve opinion until we had a chance to analyze the data.

At the same time, Lisa and Dave were in room 418 looking for the ghostly kids who had been reported playing ball up there. Among his many talents, Dave is a really clever magician. He announced that he had a ball that imparted superpowers to whoever touches it, then asked the kids to roll the ball across the floor for him.

Unfortunately, nothing happened. However, the night was still young, and Dave wasn't easily discouraged. There was a lot more to investigate.

By then, Brian and Steve had started checking out room 412, where more than one guest had reported feeling the bed shake. Steve, who was planning on spending the night there, lay down for a moment to see if there was any truth to the stories. For a while, nothing happened.

"Show yourself," Steve said. "You shook the bed a couple of days ago. Why can't you do it again?"

As if in answer to his challenge, the bed started to tremble beneath him.

But that wasn't the strangest phenomenon he and Brian would experience in that room. No sooner had Steve reported the tremor in the bed than Brian saw a shadow come up next to Steve—a shadow that looked a lot like a human hand.

"There's somebody here, Steve," Brian rasped, trying to contain his excitement.

Steve followed Brian's gaze—and saw something as well.

It was a black shadow in the corner beside the bed, as if someone was crouching there. Brian and Steve tried to catch it on camera, but by the time they reacted it was already gone.

They were understandably pumped by the experience. However, they had been in T.A.P.S. long enough to know the kinds of questions they had to ask themselves. Had a gust of wind moved the curtains, making it appear as if there had been a shadow? Could another gust have made the bed shake?

As Steve and Brian pondered those questions, Grant and I were making our way down to the hotel's basement. On more than one occasion, employees had reported feeling something tugging at their clothes down there. Suddenly, we heard a knocking sound. Tracing it to its source, we found ourselves confronted by a padlocked door.

The way my mind works, I couldn't help thinking there was someone on the other side trying to get out.

Steve and Brian, meanwhile, had made their way to the infamous room 217, where Mrs. Wilson was supposed to have unpacked Stephen King's bags. "Give us a sign," they asked, scanning the place with their instruments. No answer.

Around 5:30 a.m. we called it quits for the night. However, we left our cameras running in room 401, where I was planning on hitting the hay. This was the place where the guy had supposedly lost his jewelry to a ghost. It didn't take me long to fall into a deep sleep.

But I wasn't destined to sleep for long, because a few minutes later I heard something—the sound of the closet door opening and closing, and what sounded like conversation. Getting up out of bed, I went to check the closet door. It was open all right. But that wasn't the only thing in the room that had changed.

I always take a pill in the morning to address a chronic acid reflux problem. That means I've always got a glass beside my bed, whether I'm at home or on the road. This night was no different.

But while I was sleeping, the glass had shattered—and not in the usual way. It hadn't fallen and hit something. It had simply cracked, popping out a single jagged piece, as if pressure had expanded it from the inside.

Part of me wanted to stay awake and think about what had happened. However, I knew I had another night's investigation ahead of me. If I didn't sleep, I'd be dead to the world. So I moved the camera to cover the closet door, crawled back into bed, and drifted off.

For all of nine minutes.

By 5:48 I was up again, wakened by a new set of sounds. There was so much banging in the closet, it sounded like there was a party in there. Yet when I checked it out, there was nothing to be seen.

One phenomenon that didn't make it into the TV show took place in Grant's hotel room. Whenever he went to pull the drapes closed so he could change his clothes, they sprang open again the width of a key card. It was kind of frustrating.

But that wasn't the full extent of the problem—because one time when he closed the drapes and turned around for a second to do something, they sprang open again. And not just a little. They opened all the way.

He had never seen drapes do that before, but there's a

first time for everything. So he pulled them closed and went to the bathroom. But when he came out, the drapes were wide open again.

Now his curiosity was on high alert. He closed the drapes again, then sat down on the bed and watched television. But at the same time he was keeping an eye on the drapes, waiting for them to pop open. For twenty minutes, nothing happened. At that point, he gave up and turned to his computer bag.

That's when he heard it—the sound of the drapes hissing along their track. When he turned around, they were open all the way again.

Our second night in the hotel hit its first nugget of activ-

GRANT'S TAKE

It was weird that the drapes waited to open until I was looking the other way. Of course, it could have been just a coincidence. But to me, it seemed there was an intelligence behind the phenomenon—and a playful intelligence at that.

---

ity while Brian was setting up the mini DVR camera in room 1302. He was halfway through when he heard a man's voice whispering to him. Looking around, he tried to find the source of it, but there was no one there.

"Hello?" he called. "Hello?"

Then he heard it again. But as before, he couldn't find anyone who might have made the noise.

A little while later, Grant and I found ourselves in the

basement of the Concert Hall, checking out the concierge's claims that the place was haunted by the spirit of the homeless woman. Listening closely, we heard what sounded like footsteps and running water. Were there people in the building? Icemakers? We hoped to find out.

Two hours into the investigation, Steve and Brian walked into the MacGregor Room—and got EMF readings that were off the charts. The lowest one was over 9.0, the highest one 53.4! (Compare that to a baseline reading of 1.0!)

Steve pointed to the floor. There had to be something underneath it if he and Brian were getting a reading that incredibly high. More than likely, an electrical source. Brian went down to the basement to check it out. It didn't take long for him to find the reason for all the electromagnetic activity—a communications junction. And not a small one. It served the entire hotel.

By that time, Grant and I were examining room 401, where I had slept—or tried to—the night before. The broken drinking glass was still there, with a fragment popped out of it. Neither of us could figure out how it had happened, much less how the closet door had opened on its own.

At about 1:00, some four hours into the investigation, Brian and Steve made their way to the Billiard Room, where Mr. Stanley supposedly made an appearance from time to time. They were taking EMF readings when Brian swore and pointed to a French door—at which point Steve swung his flashlight in that direction.

By that time, there was no one there. But Brian claimed he had seen someone standing by the door until Steve's light had chased the figure away. They examined the hall-way beyond the door.

"Can you give us a sign of your presence?" Steve asked. "Can you make a noise?"

As if on cue, they heard something—the sound of a doorknob jiggling. "Did you hear that?" Brian whispered and began moving toward the noise.

"Go slow," Steve cautioned him. "Go slow."

It seemed to be an outside door that had made the noise, so they went out into the cold. But there was no one there.

About that same time, Grant hooked up with Lisa and Dave and told them he wanted to check out the stage in the MacGregor Room. Lisa and Dave followed Grant into the room, intending to scan the place with their instruments—until Grant pulled aside a curtain on the stage. Suddenly, there was a face poking through a hole in a half-shattered door—a face with a maniacal grin, a lot like Nicholson's in *The Shining*. As it happened, the face was *mine,* but that didn't stop Lisa and Dave from jumping a mile into the air, scared out of their wits.

The door to room 217—not to mention the hatchet in my hand—were props left over from the TV miniseries. It was a good joke, if I say so myself. After all our hard work, it loosened everybody up.

When the hooting and jeering were over, I told Brian I wanted him to come with me to get another look at the Concert Hall. He looked surprised. After all, I work with Grant most of the time if I work with anybody, and Brian usually winds up with Steve or somebody else. But this time was different.

It was cold outside as we left the main building, but as residents of Rhode Island we weren't exactly strangers to cold. We just put up our hoods and made our way to the Concert Hall, our breath freezing on the air like tiny wraiths.

When we got inside, we listened for sounds. One of the claims the hotel staff had made was that there was a screeching noise in the hall. We wanted to see if we had the same experience. We waited for a while, but nothing happened.

Then I broached the real reason I had asked Brian to accompany me to the Concert Hall. The guy was like a little brother to me, and had been since he joined T.A.P.S. in the early days. Yet his presence on the team had always been a source of annoyance to me and others, and his girlfriend had distracted him with her cell phone calls to the point where he had become a burden.

When he left, it was more of a relief than anything else. Then he had asked to come back and we had accepted him— against our better judgment. But it was clear to everyone, including him, that he was unofficially on probation. After being back for a while, he deserved to know where he stood.

"So," he said as we sat in the balcony, listening for anything even vaguely like a screeching noise, "how am I doing?"

I felt good being able to tell him, "Pretty good. To be honest, I didn't want to see you come back, but you live for this."

We talked about how he had gotten his life together, putting some money in the bank for a change. He wasn't a kid anymore. He was twenty-nine years old. It was time to grow up, I told him.

"I know," said Brian. He went on to tell me how much he appreciated the opportunity to rejoin the team.

I could have said that he had shown us what we wanted

to see, and that he could feel secure in his position with us, but I didn't. I knew Brian well enough to understand he needed me to be real with him.

"Don't shut the door again," I told him. "Prove me right." I had taken some heat from Grant and the rest of the team when I'd suggested we return Brian to the fold. Now he had to show us he was a changed man, not just for a moment but for the long haul.

It was a good conversation. Brian seemed to feel good hearing what I had to say. It had to be a load off his mind to know we were pleased with him.

Grant, meanwhile, was working with Dave and Lisa. They were going from guest room to guest room, trying to see if they felt anything. As I've said before, we depend heavily on our instruments for verification of our experiences, but we all go by our feelings as well.

None of the guest rooms seemed promising to them until they got to room 1302. Then they all felt something. By then, it was about 3:30 a.m. and we were seven hours into the investigation, so everyone was a little tired. But that wasn't why Lisa took the opportunity to lie down on the bed. She wanted to relax so she could open herself up to any presences in the room.

Dave said he had a feeling that they were being watched. They asked if there was anyone else in the room with them, hoping to get a ghostly response. But it was very quiet.

Grant's tape was coming to an end in his mini digital video recorder, so he went over to a heavy wooden table to change it. But it was dark in the room so Kendall Whelpton, one of our camera operators, went over to lend Grant the illumination from his camera's LCD screen.

Suddenly the whole table lifted up and slammed down—right along with the chair that was standing beside it. The movement and the resulting bang were enough to get Grant's heart pounding in his chest, and with all he's been through over the years he doesn't shock easily.

In the wake of that bang, he looked around, searching for an explanation. It occurred to him that Kendall could have moved the table with his leg as he brought his camera over, but the table was too heavy to be budged that way.

Kendall was just standing there with his mouth open, not knowing what to say. Clearly, the table had assumed a new position in the room. That much was evident from the tape Kendall had taken previously.

It was at that point that Brian and I got there and heard the story. Brian noted that he had heard a man's voice in that part of the room during his travels earlier in the evening.

Unfortunately, Dave hadn't seen the table move. He was looking in another direction at the time, so he had only heard it. Disappointed, he lingered in the room, accompanied by Steve. "It's all patience," Steve told him.

Steve's first experience was in a cemetery, but after that he didn't have one for almost five years. He knew how Dave felt. Chances to witness paranormal phenomena up close were few and far between. It was frustrating to have something take place a few feet away and not get to see it.

Trying to console Dave, Steve told him he had come a long way. Dave said that he appreciated the opportunity T.A.P.S. had given him. After all, ghost hunting was his passion in life. Finally, the edge taken off his disappointment, Dave followed Steve out of the guest room.

As for Kendall, who *had* seen the table move, his whole

view of the paranormal had changed. Prior to that night, he'd been a skeptic. He had wanted proof—and now he had gotten it. "I'm a believer now," he said, still a little shaken from the experience.

Though it was too late for us to keep investigating, we left our instruments up and rolling the rest of the night. Lisa would have to go home the next morning, but the rest of the team would stay in the hotel to analyze the data we had collected and conduct some local research.

The first apparent evidence Steve and Dave came across was the pattern of three lights that Grant and I had discovered in the MacGregor Room. At the time, we had entertained the idea that the lights were a reflection but rejected it. On the tape, however, it was clear that the lights were moving with the camera, so Steve and Dave concluded that they were a reflection after all.

Next they reviewed the tape of my experience in room 401. Though everything that happened initially was off-camera, you could clearly hear the door open and then the glass shattering. It was a good thing I moved the camera at that point to train it on the closet door, because we got the door moving and latching on tape.

We weren't so fortunate when it came to our digital video recorder or the wireless audio we had set up outside Brian's room. The moving table had eluded us as well. All we could see on the tape was the tabletop.

But Brian got something when he went to visit the Stanley Museum. The guy who runs it gave him some interesting geological information. Armed with that and the data we had recorded, we went to see hotel management with our findings.

At the meeting, Grant and I met Nancy Baker, the hotel's controller, who was interested to hear what we had to say. Billy Ward was there as well, as congenial as ever. We started out by telling them that we had been able to explain a few of the hotel's claims without resorting to the paranormal.

First, we talked about the Concert Hall. We found that if the door is open just right and the wind is blowing, it sounds like a woman screeching. Given those circumstances, we didn't believe there was any ghostly activity in the hall.

In room 412, the headboard was loose. When the window was open, the headboard could catch the wind and shiver violently enough to make the bed shake. Despite what Brian and Steve had seen, we couldn't say there was anything out of the ordinary in that room either.

The same went for the banging on the fourth floor. When we looked into it, we found that the heating pipes made a dink, dink, dink, BANG sound whenever they expanded. As plumbers, we run into that a lot. In any case, the banging wasn't attributable to any paranormal entities.

We had also raised questions about the stolen-wedding-ring claim. Though we had left some jewelry on the nightstand beside the bed in 401 for two nights running, nothing had happened to it. (But then, so much else had gone on there, the resident spirit might have been too busy to worry about a few baubles.)

An interesting footnote was Brian's discovery that the hotel was built on a mountain full of quartz, a situation that is believed to facilitate residual hauntings. The energy captured by the quartz gets released when the conditions are right, allowing spirits to manifest themselves.

Then there were our personal experiences. In the hallway by the Billiard Room, Brian and Steve had seen the shadowy figure that slunk back as they approached it. And in room 1302, the table and chair had moved. We didn't have video evidence of these occurrences, but we did have audio.

The most convincing proof we had that the hotel was haunted was the video footage from the room I had slept in. After the glass broke and I repositioned the camera, we could see the closet door close and latch. Afterward, I attempted to shut the door without turning its knob. But no matter how hard I tried, it wouldn't close that way.

It was unexplainable. Add to that all the other stuff and I couldn't help pronouncing the place haunted. Grant agreed without reservation.

All in all, the Stanley Hotel was an awesome place, a once-in-a-lifetime investigation. We were glad we had made the trip. Now we were looking forward to going home to our families in Rhode Island.

GRANT'S TAKE

I've been through a lot of shocks in the course of my ghost-hunting career, but none more unexpected than that table rising up and slamming itself down on the floor. Normally, I take the paranormal in stride. This time I thought my ribs were going to break, my heart was pounding so hard.

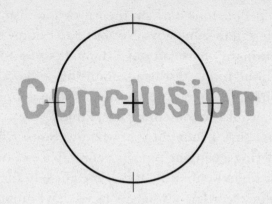

Conclusion

BY GRANT WILSON

So now what? Where do the Ghost Hunters go from here?

Our third television season is going to see us exploring a haunted castle in Ireland. You *know* we're jazzed about that. Who in their right mind wouldn't be? Afterward . . . it's hard to say. We're exploring all kinds of possibilities back at our headquarters in quaint little Warwick, Rhode Island.

It's hard to believe how far we've come since our humble beginnings in the depths of Jason's basement, when it was pretty much just the two of us going everywhere and doing everything. We never expected it to be any different—and in some ways, I guess it's not. We're still staying up late at night, crawling around in dark places full of dust and cobwebs. We're making sacrifices for the things we believe in. And we're still dedicated to our mission of putting paranormal investigation on a scientific footing, so it can finally get the respect it deserves.

Some people look back on their lives and wish they had been different in some ways. Not me, and not my friend Jason. We wouldn't have left out a thing, because without all those painful, funny, terrifying, gratifying, and occasionally awe-inspiring moments, we wouldn't be the people we are today. We would be something less, I think.

I'm not sure I thought that when we were risking our lives soldering a banging pipe in a crawl space under an old house, or when we found out that the ghost in the wall was really a tape recorder, or when we faced that inhuman entity in a supposedly empty barn. I wasn't so happy when we all got food poisoning in North Carolina, or when we had to part company—if only temporarily—with a long-standing member of our team.

But when I look back, I see how important everything was, the good times as well as the bad, and how it all fits together. I know that sounds a little touchy-feely, but hey . . . that's the kind of guy I am.

Glossary

APPARITION

A disembodied spirit visible to human beings.

ASTRAL PLANE

A level of existence separate from, and in some sense higher than, the physical world, according to certain philosophies and religious teachings.

COLD SPOT

A place that is cooler than the surrounding area. It is thought by some to be an indication of a supernatural presence drawing energy from its environment in order to manifest.

DIGITAL INFRARED CAMERA

A device used to capture images invisible to the human eye at the "hot" end of the light spectrum. It is capable of feeding information to a computer, where its infrared images may be stored on a hard drive.

DIGITAL THERMOMETER

A device used to record the presence of cold spots and hot spots, sometimes during an apparent paranormal event. Some digital thermometers record temperatures second-by-second for PC storage and graphical charting.

ECTOPLASM

A filmy, quasi-solid substance that supposedly issues from the bodies of mediums while they are in trance states. Ectoplasm may issue from the mouth, the nostrils, the eyes, the ears, the navel, or the nipples. In photographs, ectoplasm resembles muslin fabric soaked in water.

ELECTROMAGNETIC FIELD RECORDER

A device used to record data on electromagnetic fields (EMFs). Its use is controversial among ghost hunters in that EMFs from power lines, television sets, kitchen applicances, etc. surround us constantly, as well as the fact that it has yet to be categorically proven that ghosts emit EM energy. On the other hand, some researchers say ghosts disrupt EMFs.

EVP

Electronic voice phenomena. Audio devices may record disembodied voices and other supernatural sounds that are inaudible to the human ear without mechanical intervention.

EXORCISM

Ritual expulsion of invading spiritual or demonic entities from a person or dwelling. The term was brought into the common vernacular by the 1973 movie *The Exorcist.*

FLOATING ORB

A spherical image, usually a translucent white though sometimes a reddish or bluish hue, which inexplicably registers on film or videotape. Its presence is thought by some to be an indicator of supernatural activity.

GHOST

The soul or spirit of a dead person, reflecting the appearance of his or her living body but less substantial. Ghosts may exist in a state of semi-awareness or be completely cognizant of their living observers.

GHOST HUNTER/INVESTIGATOR

A person who attempts to gather evidence of ghosts or other paranormal activity. This may be accomplished by means of still photography, video, audio, EMF recordings, EVP recordings, or other media.

HAUNTING

The manifestation of a ghostly presence attached to a specific person or location.

INHUMAN ENTITY

A demon or other spirit intent on causing harm to living beings. Also known as a *negative entity.*

GLOSSARY

INTELLIGENT HAUNTING

A supernatural entity that is aware of its surroundings and/or observers and is capable of interaction with them.

MATERIALIZATION

The procedure through which a ghost appears. Materialization can be sudden or gradual, resulting in an entity that is indistinct or seemingly quite solid.

MATRIXING

The natural tendency of the human mind to add details to sensory input (perceived through the visual, auditory, olfactory, or tactile senses) so as to create a familiar or easily understood pattern. In effect, matrixing is mentally "filling in the blanks."

OUIJA BOARD

A wooden board preprinted with letters, numbers, and words used by mediums to receive supernatural communications.

PARANORMAL

The realm of occurrences and phenomena removed from those to which people are exposed in everyday experience.

PHANTOM SMELL

Any scent through which a supernatural entity is attempting to express itself. Typically, phantom smells are reminiscent of flowers, cigarettes, or perfume, but they don't come from any identifiable source.

POLTERGEIST

A ghost that manifests its presence through noises, rappings, the moving of objects, and the creation of disorder. The relocation of furniture is an indication of poltergeist activity.

RESIDUAL HAUNTING

A scene from the past that continues to be played out over and over again, like a recording, with the witness of the phenomenon essentially peering into a former era. The ghostly participants in these time displacements often seem unaware of their living observers.

SENSITIVE

A medium or clairvoyant. A sensitive can see or feel people, objects, and events in the realm of the paranormal.

THERMAL-IMAGING DIGITAL CAMERA

A device that records images of long-wavelength infrared radiation (i.e., heat) that are invisible to the human eye. The thermal-imaging camera facilitates the capture of images in darkness, smoke, or fog.

VORTEX

An anomaly that sometimes shows up in still photographs taken at the site of a suspected haunting, appearing as a translucent white tube or funnel-shaped mass. Some researchers believe vortices may be portals to the spirit realm.

The Ghost Hunter's Manual

SAFETY

There are two sources of danger in a paranormal investigation. The first kind comes in the form of physical obstacles like doors, chairs, low-hanging chandeliers, loose carpets, and rusty nails. In the light, these are easily avoided. In the dark, you can do real damage to yourself.

Always conduct a walk-through before you shut off the lights. Make note of possible hazards and share the information with everyone on your team. The last thing you want to do is interrupt a ghost hunt to drive one of your colleagues to the emergency room.

The second kind of danger is more difficult to foresee. Most of the time, the supernatural entities you will encounter are human or benign spirits. Occasionally, they will be inhuman spirits, the kind that want to do you harm. Through interviews and simple observations, try to get a sense of what kind of activity you're dealing with. Then proceed accordingly.

THE CLIENT

Always interview your client before you begin the investigation. How credible are his or her accounts? Does he or she have an agenda in asking you to hunt for ghosts on his or her property? Is this person in touch with reality?

Ghost hunters have to be careful whom they're working for. Our investigations may lead to book and movie deals, as in the case of the Amityville Horror house, or to other kinds of commercial success. What hotel or restaurant isn't going to benefit from the label "haunted"?

Still, we have to remember why we got into this business—to help people. It's better to be taken advantage of than to walk out on a person who might sincerely need your assistance. When in doubt, take the client's word at face value.

EVIDENCE

As we have noted, some investigators are content to base their assesments on their feelings. If a house seems haunted to them, they believe they have done their job and can declare it haunted. We approach ghost hunting from a scientific point of view.

The only kind of evidence we accept is the kind that can be examined by others, whether it's a still photograph, a video recording, or an audio recording. If other people can't go over it and come to the same conclusions we did, it's not proof as far as we're concerned. Therefore, we go to great lengths to ensure the integrity of our documentation.

That starts with our policy to keep the client separate from the investigation. Once we turn our cameras on, we don't want anyone except a member of our team going near them. That way, no one can say the evidence was tampered with. Only after the data has been thoroughly analyzed do we share it with the client.

It is also important to have your investigators work in pairs. Paranormal experiences are difficult to come by. When they happen, you want more than one person on hand to witness it. There's a safety issue here as well. If someone is hurt or endangered, you want a colleague on hand to help or call for assistance.

Identify the naturally occurring sources of noise and light in the venue under investigation. These can affect the integrity of your evidence. What sounds like growling might be an old heating system turning on and off.

Log everything in detail, including fleeting sensations. Later on, it may be difficult for you to remember what happened and in what sequence. By keeping a log, you give yourself a chance to re-create events as they occurred.

Subject any anomalies you may have captured to various modes of processing in order to clarify their nature or to debunk them. In other words, use different kinds of equipment in the same areas. If you picked up a strange image in a bedroom, take some EMF readings there as well, or try scanning with a thermal-imaging camera.

Even after you've analyzed the data, your job isn't over.

Return to the place where you captured the anomalies, replicate as closely as possible the conditions under which you were operating, and try to come up with an alternative explanation. If you can do so, you may not have legitimate evidence after all.

PROFESSIONAL DEMEANOR

No matter what you see or hear, be professional. Whatever your feelings may be, keep them in check. Act responsibly so the other members of your team know they can count on you.

Paranormal investigations aren't slumber parties. They're attempts to help real people with real problems. Remember, it's not just your own reputation on the line—it's the reputation of all ghost hunters everywhere.

DEALING WITH SPIRITS

When attempting to communicate with supernatural entities, observe what has become the established protocol. Speak clearly and in a relaxed fashion. Try not to let eagerness or anxiety get in the way. If you were a spirit, what kind of living person would you want to speak with? More than likely, one who is calm, unhurried, and in control of his or her emotions.

After you ask a question, wait a few moments. The spirit you're addressing may not be able to answer as quickly as you would like. Give him or her time. Then, if you haven't detected a response, ask another question.

SELF-CONTROL

The scientific approach demands one thing above all else: objectivity. If you're going to conduct a reliable investigation, you can't give in to preconceptions. You've got to check them at the door.

In some cases, you will be investigating sites with long histories of supernatural activity attached to them. It's tempting to go in trying to add to these histories. However, you've got to treat every venue as if you've never heard of it before.

Always try to find a natural explanation before accepting a paranormal one. Let's face it: paranormal occurrences are rare. Most of the time—eighty percent, in our experience—what seems like a ghostly voice is only a cranky waste pipe.

Whether you're observing phenomena firsthand or analyzing them afterward, you have to be careful of matrixing. The human mind is a helpful organ. If you let it, it will show you exactly what you want to see—as opposed to what's actually there.

Then there's the client. It's only natural for ghost hunters to want to appease him or her, even if he or she's not paying them. After all, clients are nice people. They're inviting you into their homes. You don't want to disappoint them.

However, you're not doing anyone a service by making claims without evidence to back them up. The homeowner has a right to know the truth. If you don't find anything, say so.